"Where are we going now?"

"To Quito," Vicente answered curtly. "Contrary to the plans you and my father devised, I have no intention of playing tour guide again."

"Plans your father and I...? I knew nothing about this trip until this morning."

"No, of course not," he said sarcastically. "He dreamed all this up by himself." Vicente gave her a suspicious glance. "I have no idea how you manipulated my father so easily, but he certainly seems captivated by you."

"Manip— You're the one who's been doing the manipulating. Right from the moment you met me at the airport."

He ignored the comment. "We'll arrive in half an hour. Will that be quick enough for you?"

"The question should be, 'Is that quick enough for *you?*'" she retorted, then turned her head to stare out the window. *And don't worry—I promise, soon you'll be free of my company forever.*

Kate Denton is a pseudonym for the Texas writing team of Carolyn Hake and Jeanie Lambright. Friends as well as coauthors, they concur for the most part on politics and good Mexican restaurants, but disagree about men—tall versus short—and what constitutes good weather—sun versus showers. One thing they definitely agree on is the importance of romance.

Books by Kate Denton

CROSS PURPOSES
Kate Denton

Harlequin Books

TORONTO • NEW YORK • LONDON
AMSTERDAM • PARIS • SYDNEY • HAMBURG
STOCKHOLM • ATHENS • TOKYO • MILAN
MADRID • WARSAW • BUDAPEST • AUCKLAND

To Cecilia de Freire of Quito, Ecuador—in appreciation
of your assistance and hospitality

ISBN 0-373-03332-X

CROSS PURPOSES

Copyright © 1994 by Kate Denton.

PROLOGUE

ALEX TOSSED her glasses onto the desk and massaged the bridge of her nose, then she raked her fingers through her already tousled blond hair. How had she gotten coerced into taking this assignment?

A tree branch scratching against the window of her second-floor study caught her attention, and she turned her head toward the sound. Oklahoma City was in the grip of a blustery norther today, fierce winds stripping the trees and bushes of any remaining stubborn foliage. Alex felt as if her mind was being buffeted in the same fashion.

Her problems had started with a chance comment to an editor of *Newsmakers* magazine. He'd been on campus to give a lecture to a class of journalism students and afterward had dropped by the Spanish Department to visit an old friend. The old friend happened to be Alex's adviser on her doctoral dissertation. During their reminiscing, Alex had popped in and been introduced, and Dr. Hanson had mentioned that the author Camila Zavala was the subject of Alex's dissertation. Before she knew it, the two men had decided that Alex should do a story on Camila for *Newsmakers*.

Certainly such an article would be a coup for the university. Camila Zavala, the "Angel of the Andes," was earning rave reviews and even being touted in some circles as a Nobel Prize contender. And Alex probably knew more about the author than anyone else in the U.S.—with the exception of Camila's publisher. But Alex was an academic, not a reporter.

And she suspected Bill Briggs, the *Newsmakers* editor, wanted something more than just dry research. When would she learn how to say no? She picked up her glasses again, remembering that she *had* said no—only to be overruled by Dr. Hanson.

She stared at the dust jacket of Camila's latest book, *Death of the Amazon.* Her curiosity had been piqued as soon as she'd started reading the first page. All those satisfying hours previously invested in Camila's work were now transforming into periods of doubt. Camila's writing had changed. Alex could not ignore or understand the differences in style between this book and the writer's earlier efforts.

It was those differences that intrigued Bill Briggs. Now that the book was being so well received by the public, Alex wasn't the only one who had questions. "Zavala's been a fairly obscure writer up to this point," Bill had said, "but this book's going to hit the top of the bestseller list and sit there awhile. What's so different about this one? And why won't she consent to an interview? We need to scoop the competition, be the first to answer those questions."

Scoop? Answer? How could she be expected to explain the change in Camila Zavala's work when she hadn't yet gotten a grasp on it herself?

"How's it going?" Scott Harper's words snapped Alex out of her reverie. Placing his luggage at the door of Alex's study, he walked over to scan the screen of his daughter's word processor. "Not well, I see. Isn't that where you stopped yesterday—with the title?"

"Suffice to say I've hit an impasse with the article," Alex grumbled. "I'm so confused I can't concentrate on my dissertation, either." She uncurled her legs from those of the chair and stood up to stretch. Reaching for the carafe on the desk, she poured another cup of coffee, her fourth that morning. "Something's definitely not right. I read the book again, just like you suggested, hoping I'd find some answers. It didn't work." She raised the cup to her lips, then put it down with a grimace. The coffee was tepid.

Scott squeezed Alex's shoulder affectionately. "But you've maintained all along Camila's writing was changing, that her previous book was different, too. I thought you'd decided she was simply maturing."

"True, but in spite of the changes, that other book, those words were—how can I explain—still Camila's." She picked up a copy of the novel on her desk. "These words seem to have come from someone else entirely."

"Are you sure it's the novel and not you? Maybe Camila's decision to stop corresponding is clouding your thinking." Scott Harper's full ruddy face eased into a sympathetic but questioning smile. "Speaking of the letters, why don't you use some of them for the article?" Without waiting for a response, he hurried toward the door. "Gotta get packed, hon. I'm off to St. Louis." Pondering his suggestion, Alex absent-mindedly reached for her coffee cup again.

Could she use Camila's letters? Perhaps. But she wasn't sure she really wanted to. After all, they'd been her secret up to this point, she hadn't even mentioned them to Dr. Hanson. Only her family had known of the connection. To the modest Alex, publicizing the fact that she and Camila Zavala had been pen pals would have been nothing short of bragging. Exposing private correspondence for career reasons didn't sit well with her.

Alex rummaged through a box of folders under her desk and pulled out a small packet of letters. According to the last postmark, almost two years had passed since she'd heard from the writer, each month of silence having increased Alex's feelings of rejection. And when Alex heard there would be no more, it was as though she'd been forsaken by a friend.

In truth, the letters had not been personally revealing, but rather a warm exchange between a famous author and a fan, primarily a telling of tales, occasionally a sharing of thoughts and ideas. Alex removed the last letter from its envelope and stared down at Camila's elegant script. This one was like the others—filled with colorful vignettes of life in another country, stories that might find their way into a future Camila novel.

Alex had always responded quickly, aware of the several weeks needed for the mail to wend its way from the publisher in New York to Camila's home in the small South American country of Ecuador. Camila had been an equally conscientious correspondent, never allowing more than a month or two to go by without answering. As a result, Alex had heard from the writer about twice a year.

But a time came when Camila had failed to answer. After almost a year passed with no word, Alex wrote her again. It had taken a third effort before she'd finally received a reply from the publisher informing her of Camila's desire that no more mail be forwarded. Coincidentally, that letter had arrived the same day *Death of the Amazon* hit the bookstores.

Before the appearance of the novel, Alex had worried that she'd somehow offended Camila. Now she wasn't sure what to think. *Death of the Amazon* was stirring—probably Camila's best effort—yet it had a decidedly different feel from the others, especially her earliest novels. Alex feared there might be something wrong with Camila. But what? And what could she do about it, anyway?

Alex tapped a fingernail on the packet of letters. She'd felt close to Camila, felt as if she knew her, but now those emotions seemed naive and presumptuous as Alex realized that, despite the letters, she really didn't know Camila Zavala at all. Perhaps the time had come to get better acquainted. She turned toward her father who'd reappeared in the doorway.

"What I'd really like to do," she said, "is go to Ecuador and try to meet Camila. I want answers for myself, not just for the *Newsmakers* article."

"Then do it," Scott said.

Alex sighed. "You don't think I'm being silly? Unrealistic?"

"So what if you are? Go for it. Honey, I'm sure *Newsmakers* would finance such a trip."

"Oh, maybe it's impossible, anyway. Except for her mention of a house in Quito, I don't know where to find Camila. Quito has a population of a million-plus people, so it's a pretty formidable place to go blindly searching for someone."

"What are you trying to do? Talk yourself out of it? You're not making much progress here—" Scott gestured toward the blank computer screen "—so perhaps a change of scenery will help. And perhaps you will meet Camila."

"My father, the eternal optimist."

"No, just a man who has confidence in his daughter's abilities. You're fluent in Spanish. You know how to research. Plus, you're the most determined hardheaded person I've ever met."

"Like father, like daughter."

Scott shrugged, then continued. "Don't forget, I have a few contacts in Ecuador." Traveling on behalf of his oil-field equipment company, her father had made several trips there. "Check my Rolodex and give the Serranos a call. Maybe they can help." He rested a hip on the corner of her desk. "I don't know if you realize it, but Juan Carlos Serrano is sort of responsible for your interest in Camila. On my first trip to Ecuador, I mentioned that I wanted to bring you some books written by Ecuadorans. He's the one who suggested Camila." Scott looked at his watch, then kissed her cheek. "I'd better run. My flight's in less than an hour."

Alex tried to work for the remainder of the morning, but she couldn't dismiss the idea of actually visiting Ecuador. She'd always been fascinated with the country, its allure growing with Scott's stories of his travels and Camila's books and letters. Why shouldn't she go? Her passport was current, and she had enough money in her savings account to finance a trip, so she didn't need help or permission from *Newsmakers*. A few phone calls, a couple of vaccinations and she could be on her way. She had a month to finish the magazine article. Maybe a little extra inspiration would be the key to meeting that deadline.

"The Serranos," Alex said aloud. She descended the stairs and went into the den, seeking family photo albums. Scott Harper had last visited Ecuador only the year before and had brought back snapshots.

She opened an album and flipped through the pages until she found what she was looking for. Scott seldom took photographs while on business, but because of his daughter's fascination with Camila he'd taken a camera to Ecuador. Most of his shots were landscapes—generally out of focus, thanks to Scott's ineptness as a photographer—but one photo showed Scott and two special clients.

Alex removed the picture and read the writing on the back. "Vicente and Juan Carlos Serrano." Just as she'd thought. Then she'd made her decision. She would go to South America and seek out Camila Zavala. And if she failed? Well, it wouldn't be a total loss—at least she'd return with valuable background material for her dissertation and the article. Confident that she'd soon have her answers, Alex replaced the photo and headed back upstairs in search of her father's Rolodex.

CHAPTER ONE

"BUENAS TARDES, SEÑORITA." The uniformed customs agent briefly studied her passport, stamped it, then handed it back. "Welcome to Ecuador."

"Gracias," Alex said, tucking the passport into her purse and moving toward the carousel in search of her luggage. She located her suitcase and garment bag, hefted them aboard a cart and trudged toward customs. A half hour later, she was standing outside the terminal wondering how one went about hailing a taxi in Quito.

"Señorita Harper?"

"Yes?" Alex's voice was a high-pitched squeak, a startled reaction to the man standing in front of her.

"Vicente Serrano at your service," he announced. His English was perfect, with only a trace of a Spanish accent.

Vicente Serrano! What was he doing here? This was embarrassing. Alex hadn't anticipated him—or anyone, for that matter—showing up to greet her. Had her call to the Serrano residence created the impression that she expected to be met?

She'd phoned her father's business associates days ago, explaining to Juan Carlos Serrano, Vicente's father, that she was writing a magazine article and would be making a research visit to their country. She hadn't mentioned the topic of the article, nor asked for help in locating Camila. It seemed overly familiar to do so. Her father's business connection notwithstanding, she was a stranger to the Serranos. So she'd only sought advice on hotel and travel arrangements during the brief conversation. No further assistance had been requested. Or so she'd thought.

"How do you do," she said, extending a hand and fighting back a blush of self-consciousness.

Like most Ecuadorans, Vicente was dark, with hair as rich as polished ebony and dark brown, almost black eyes. His complexion was a deep tan—a shade many pale Americans paid countless dollars to achieve in tanning salons. He wasn't tall, perhaps only five foot ten, but he seemed much taller than his fellow countrymen who were rushing about them.

Alex slowly began to comprehend that she should have foreseen an appearance by a Serrano. The Ecuadorans were by reputation a gracious people, and good manners dictated unquestioning courtesy. Still the encounter unnerved her in more ways than one.

The picture in the family album had shown Vicente to be handsome. The man in the photograph, however, and the flesh-and-blood male smiling at her now from a few feet away were light-years apart—the intense masculinity he exuded obviously impossible to capture on film.

"You shouldn't have gone to this trouble," she protested. "I could have caught a cab."

"Oh, but I could not let you make your way alone." He smiled, dimples showing in his smooth skin. "I plan to assist you in every way possible." Without waiting for assent, he took the suitcase and garment bag from her hands. "My car's this way," he said, and began crossing the street.

Alex stared for an instant, then hurried to catch up as Vicente strode to a nearby parking lot. He stopped at a cream-colored Audi, opened the door and motioned her inside, then put her bags and the laptop computer she'd been carrying into the trunk. Within minutes they were maneuvering through the hectic Quito traffic.

As they sped along, she turned her head from side to side to take in the sights, intrigued by the contrasts of the city—stucco buildings standing alongside those of glass and steel, upstart high rises dwarfing centuries-old colonial churches.

The scene called to mind cities in Spain she'd visited with her family, and Alex was slightly surprised to discover the same eclectic mix of old and new. *What were you expecting?* she asked herself. *Primitive huts and llamas tied to hitching posts?*

"You must be tired after your journey," Vicente commented, glancing her way.

"A little," she said. "I'm glad there's only an hour's difference in time zones. At least I don't have to cope with jet lag, too."

"Still it's a long trip. I know from my own experience."

"When were you last in the States?"

"A couple of months ago. I travel mostly to Miami or New York. In fact, I happened upon your father at the Miami airport then."

Alex smiled knowingly. "It doesn't surprise me that you spotted him at an airport. He seems to spend more time running for flights than he does at home. We try to get him to slow down, but..." She shrugged in frustration.

"I understand completely. My father has begun to reduce his activities only recently, since my mother's death. He's semiretired now and passing most of his days at our hacienda in the country. By the way, he insisted I bring you for a visit before you return home. He said he enjoyed his brief phone conversation with the 'charming Señorita Harper' and wants to meet you in person."

"That would be nice," Alex said agreeably, all the while wondering the best way to refuse. She'd come to Ecuador to work, not to socialize. Besides, she couldn't impose on the Serranos any more than she already had. After Vicente dropped her off at the hotel, she'd make a note to herself to send a small thank-you gift, and then decline all future invitations.

Alex noticed they had left the commercial district and were now driving in a residential area. Her confusion intensified as Vicente turned off the main street, easing the car through a pair of wrought-iron gates and into a paved courtyard. She looked around. "Where are we?"

"Casa Serrano—my home. I decided you'd be much more comfortable here than at the hotel."

A spurt of annoyance surfaced. She knew South American males were stereotyped as being aggressive and domineering. Vicente's changing her lodging without even consulting her seemed to confirm this reputation. "I think I'd be more comfortable at the hotel," she said. "If it isn't convenient for you to take me there, then I'll use your phone to call a taxi."

Vicente studied her quietly. "I've upset you, and I apologize for rearranging your plans," he said placatingly. "But my father—and I also—would feel remiss as hosts if you didn't stay at our home. Hotel rooms in strange countries are so solitary, so impersonal. And you don't have to worry about impropriety—naturally, we won't be alone. My father's at the hacienda, but we have a housekeeper and a cook here, as well as two gardeners."

She didn't speak, so he continued. "I'm sure you and your family would do the same if I was visiting Oklahoma." Vicente smiled, the sort of charming smile that Alex was sure allowed him to have his way in most arguments, particularly those with women.

Even as she felt manipulated, Alex didn't wish to appear ungracious. The man's intentions were probably good, and she had to keep in mind that customs here were different. To refuse their hospitality would be an insult to an influential family like the Serranos—and unwise, too. It was time to start thinking like a reporter. After all, she had an article to write and might need their assistance later. Vicente Serrano's cooperation could prove essential if she was to succeed in her quest to find Camila. "I don't want to be a bother," she protested mildly.

"How could a beautiful woman ever be a bother?" His voice was low and husky, almost a caress, before abruptly returning to its formal tone. "Now, let's have no more resistance." He stepped out of the car and motioned to one of the gardeners who was turning the soil in a bed of bold pink geraniums. The man dropped his tools and cleaned his hands at an outdoor faucet before coming to carry her luggage inside.

Alex glanced around as she followed the two men. The home sat atop a hilly street similar to those in San Francisco. In fact, the house itself reminded her of something she'd see in California—large and bright and breezy with whitewashed stucco walls and a rust red tile roof.

A housekeeper in a crisp black uniform met them in the hall. She was short and slender, probably in her midforties, and her dark hair was tightly pulled into a neat bun. "Señor Serrano. *Bienvenida, señorita.*" She gave Alex a slight curtsy.

In Spanish Vicente said, "Luisa, please show Miss Harper to her suite."

He turned to Alex. "There is a bedroom and bath with an adjoining study where you can work. Why don't you relax for a few hours, then we'll go out for dinner.''

"Thanks, but it's not necessary for you to chauffeur me around. I'm sure you probably have more important matters to take care of.''

"What could be more important? Besides, the reservations are already made.''

Alex gave him a weak smile. "In that case, dinner sounds lovely.'' Even as she acquiesced, Alex was growing more surprised and slightly irritated, too, at his presumptuous behavior. She'd traveled here on business, not pleasure, and couldn't afford to have someone dominating her agenda to the exclusion of everything else. Then again, maybe she was overreacting. She'd been in Quito only a short time, too soon to complain about a surplus of attention. "I'll need an hour or so to unpack and freshen up. And I want to telephone my family to let them know about the change in plans.''

"Of course. There's no hurry. I'll be in my study attending to some paperwork. Shall we say eight for dinner?''

Alex talked briefly with her sister, Margaret, and put her belongings away before filling the sumptuous sunken tub for a leisurely bath. As she was soaking, she deliberated over this unexpected turn of events. Vicente Serrano apparently had a strong sense of obligation, misguided though it was. The question was, how far did that obligation take him? He knew she had work to do. He'd indicated as much when he'd arranged to have a study for her use. Perhaps he intended to leave her to her own devices after this initial round of welcoming. The thought was comforting, and she closed her eyes to relax awhile before climbing out of the tub and getting dressed.

She was uncertain what to wear. The weather had been mild on her arrival, but Alex recalled that the guidebook she'd read had said the evenings became quite cool. She settled on a mint green skirt with a matching print blouse and a jacket-style sweater. After dressing, she applied fresh makeup and released her honey blond hair from the clip that had held it up.

A short time later Alex and Vicente were riding in an elevator, which was taking them to the top floor of the Hotel Quito. The restaurant was elegant—tuxedoed waiters moved amid white-clothed tables adorned with bowls of fresh flowers, and there was a magnificent view of the city. Lights twinkled from houses built onto the sides of the mountains in seeming defiance of the laws of gravity.

"The view of the city is spectacular."

"Quito is quite special," Vicente said proudly. "Museums, historical sites, parks. This is your first visit, I understand."

"Yes, but I'm somewhat familiar with your country through my studies."

"Of course. I recall Scott saying that your doctoral thesis is on South American literature."

Alex nodded.

"But you're here to do research for a magazine article?"

"That's right, and I must admit I'm a little nervous about it. Camila Zavala's the subject of my dissertation and since her new book has attracted so much notice, I've been asked to do a profile on her for *Newsmakers*. Are you familiar with the magazine?"

"Sí." A cloud passed over Vicente's face, disappearing so quickly Alex wondered if she'd imagined it. "And how do you approach something like that?" he asked. The question was cordial, but his expression was wary, almost distrustful.

"Frankly I'm not sure," Alex answered, deciding that she wanted to find out why he seemed displeased with her topic. She suspected she knew. Vicente Serrano came from a wealthy traditional family. He probably sided with the conservative forces who opposed the costly reforms advocated by Camila. Any additional publicity for the author, especially favorable publicity, would be unwelcome.

"I suppose I'll start with the university," she continued cautiously, "and check out the library there. I also want to visit some of the places Camila has described in her books to get a feel for them."

There was a long silence during which Vicente appeared to be considering her plans. Then the waiter approached their table with a bottle of wine and poured a little into Vicente's glass. After the ritual sampling, he filled both glasses. "It's Chilean, one of my favorites," Vicente told her.

Alex approved of his selection, a dry, light-bodied rosé. It was the perfect tonic after a long day of travel.

"Shall we order?"

She opened the menu, gaped at what she saw, then chuckled.

"Something amusing?"

"Forgive me," she said. "I was shocked at first to see how high the prices are." She leaned toward Vicente, showing him the entrée she'd selected. "Thousands of *sucres*. It seems an exorbitant amount until you figure out it's only a few U.S. dollars. I was laughing at my mistake. Actually the cost is quite low."

"To you, yes. But not for Ecuadorans. Keep in mind that the majority of my countrymen earn very little. The average wage here is a mere fraction of that in the States, too modest for most to afford even this price. The Serrano family has been very fortunate. We have much to be grateful for."

The waiter reappeared and took their orders, his deference to "Señor Serrano" emphasizing just how well-off and influential the family must be.

"As I was saying, Ecuador is a poor country. And largely unrecognized, too." Vicente shook his head. "Right now, many people can't even find us on the map. But gradually we're becoming more known."

"Partly because of Camila Zavala?" she prompted, eager to bring the writer up again.

"Partly," he agreed, with a nonchalant shrug. "Camila's writing has generated much attention to our country by addressing some of the problems with the indigenous population, such as the need for better medical care and improved hygiene. But for the most part, her exposés have been about our neighboring countries." He studied Alex carefully. "I'm curious about your choice. Why Camila Zavala? South America has produced writers more famous—Gabriel García Marquez or Isabel Allende, for example."

Alex nodded. "Over the long term maybe more famous. But at the moment no one is more newsworthy or creating greater dissention than Zavala. The environmental movement is growing stronger all the time. Maybe that's the reason her latest book about the exploitation of the rain forests is becoming so popular."

"Is that why you've decided to devote your dissertation to her? To write magazine articles about her? Perhaps you wish to exploit Camila?"

"Never," she said defensively, concluding that she really didn't care much for Vicente Serrano. "My interest was formed long before *Death of the Amazon* was released. I respect Camila and want to engender the same feelings in others."

"Why?" He looked extremely skeptical.

Alex paused, hardly knowing where to begin. There was more than professional interest here—there was also an emotional tie, one that had lasted for over a decade. Alex had initially written to Camila Zavala when she was an impressionable fourteen-year-old, encouraged by her father to reach out to her favorite author with a fan letter. Camila's second novel had inched onto the bestseller lists, so Alex had sent her a short note of congratulations. Scott may not have been surprised, but Alex was astonished when the note had been answered by Camila herself. That had been the beginning of a lengthy correspondence.

For nine years, she and Camila had exchanged letters, Alex saving and savoring every one. The letters, not the writer's growing popularity, had been the basis for choosing Camila as her dissertation subject. And the offer to do the article had come to her, not vice versa. She certainly hadn't wanted—still didn't want—to write it.

But how to explain all this to someone she'd just met? She couldn't expect him to empathize with the hero worship of a young girl still smoldering years later in the heart of a grown woman. It sounded silly and immature when put into words. "Let's just say she piqued my interest."

Vicente nodded. "And that of many others, too. An unfortunate outcome, since Camila desires attention focused anywhere but on herself."

"You talk as if you know her." Alex's hopes rose.

He was quiet for long moments, as though trying to decide whether to answer. "I know of her, naturally. Everyone does. But enough of that. As I recall, you spent a year in Mexico when you were an undergraduate. Does Ecuador compare favorably?"

"How did you know?" she asked, ignoring his question.

He took a sip of wine. "Your father must have mentioned it during one of our business meetings."

"Daddy does have the habit of boring people with stories about his six daughters—and his grandchildren, too. He's the world's proudest grandfather."

"My father envies him the grandchildren. How many are there now?"

"Seven and counting. My sister Grace is expecting a baby in a couple of months. What about you? Brothers or sisters?"

"No. I'm a rarity in our society—an only child."

What about a wife? she wanted to ask. Alex had assumed Vicente was unmarried—there was no Señora Serrano on the premises and surely he wouldn't bring home a female guest with his wife away. She glanced at his hands. No wedding band, only a gold signet ring on one of his fingers. Her curiosity surprised her. Rarely did she wonder about a man's marital state. But then all during the meal she'd found herself dwelling on him—on his soft mesmerizing eyes and his appealingly dimpled smile. Obviously the wine and the altitude were making her a bit fuzzy headed. The man might look good, but there were times when his behavior bordered on rude.

The waiter's voice interrupted her reverie. *"Postre?"*

Alex started to refuse, but Vicente answered for her. "Sí. The chocolate mousse." Only then did he look at Alex for approval, and she nodded. "And coffee," he added.

They continued to talk about their families, but as soon as they were served, Alex once again brought up her favorite subject. "My fondest wish is to meet Camila Zavala. Talk with her. Do you know of any way I could make contact while I'm here?"

"That would be impossible." He shook his head emphatically. "Camila doesn't socialize. And even if she did, no one knows where to find her. As you've no doubt read, she's quite the recluse."

"So it seems." Alex didn't need Vicente telling her about Camila Zavala. She'd absorbed every piece of information published about the controversial writer. And a few things more—thanks to her letters. Camila's insistence on anonymity made Alex's problem more complex. How did you find someone who didn't want to be found?

Interviewing her would certainly enhance the *Newsmakers* profile, and since Alex had said she'd write the article, she might as well do the best job she could. But meeting Camila meant more than that—it would also fulfill a long-standing dream. Alex glanced over at Vicente. "But you must have some ideas on how to reach her."

"None at all," Vicente said. "She's never been outgoing, and after the tremendous response—both positive and negative—to this new book, it appears she's totally dropped out of circulation. She's not like your North American writers who constantly court publicity. Camila lets her novels speak for themselves." He smiled. "But again, enough about her. It's time to go. You must be tired by now." He signaled for the check.

Alex sighed. Dinner had been delicious and served in leisurely continental fashion. But while they'd talked, she'd become increasingly frustrated by Vicente's constant thwarting of her attempts to bring Camila into the conversation. She made a couple of halfhearted efforts on the drive back to Casa Serrano, efforts he deftly deflected with comments about various Quito landmarks.

They pulled inside the gate, and he followed her into the house. "Would you care for a liqueur?"

Alex groaned. "No, thank you. I've had too much to eat and drink as it is, and since I'm planning a morning trip to Otavalo, I'd better get to bed." Otavalo was one of the places she was most anxious to see. Camila had used the town as the setting for her first novel and had also described its Indian Market in a letter.

Alex would have preferred to become familiar with Quito before taking side trips, but the market was only held on Saturdays. Besides, Otavalo was convenient, accessible by bus or automobile and not far from Quito. All she needed was transportation to the rental-car agency or bus station.

She extended her hand to him. "Thank you for a lovely dinner."

Vicente bowed slightly as he grasped her hand, holding it longer than seemed necessary. Alex felt a stirring sensation, a strong awareness of his touch.

How can a handshake be sensual? she wondered. But it was, and she was relieved when he finally released her. "Good night."

"Good night. Plan on rising early. It's better to arrive in Otavalo before the tour buses."

The door of her suite closed behind her and Alex prepared for bed. She was tired, but too preoccupied to consider sleep. Yesterday she'd expected to spend the evening alone at the hotel busily planning her two-week stay in Ecuador. Instead, she was reclining against an ornately carved headboard, trying to focus her attention to Camila Zavala. For the first time in months, she was having trouble giving total concentration to the writer.

She supposed she should be grateful for the turn of events that resulted in her being the guest of someone who, despite his professed indifference, might open doors for her. But right now gratitude wasn't the overwhelming emotion she was experiencing.

Instead, her thoughts were on Vicente Serrano, and she couldn't seem to escape them. It was more than just his looks that she found arresting. There was also an indefinable, indescribable something about him that was magnetic and unsettling.

Alex had never experienced such an attraction to a man before, and she was shocked by the desire rising within her. Irritated, too, because she didn't have time for romantic nonsense. Not when there was so much work to be done.

She'd have to double her efforts to keep her attentions on her goal. Her academic successes had come about in great part because she was so single-minded, able to focus on one subject to the exclusion of everything else. She would just have to call upon that ability while she was here. And to guarantee success, she'd make sure there was sufficient geography separating her from any distractions. Especially Vicente.

CHAPTER TWO

DRESSED IN AN AQUA turtleneck and matching skirt, Alex went downstairs to the patio for breakfast. Even though it wasn't yet seven, Vicente was engaged in an animated telephone conversation. Alex paused at the open French doors, waiting for her host to finish his call.

From where she stood, it was impossible to avoid overhearing what appeared to be an apology. "But I have a guest, Silvia, a guest who's a stranger to our country. Surely you can understand that." On raising his eyes and spotting Alex, Vicente signaled her to join him. "Now I must go," he insisted, placing the cordless receiver on the table and rising from his chair.

"Buenos días," she said.

"Good morning, Alex." Vicente motioned to Luisa, who approached them with a silver pitcher of hot milk, which she poured into their cups. From a small carafe, Vicente added a splash of thick black coffee to the milk, turning the mixture a creamy beige.

Alex took a tentative sip. The drink was delicious, similar to the café au lait she'd once had in New Orleans. She picked up a roll and broke off a piece to spread with blackberry jam.

As she ate, Alex looked around the backyard—a peaceful verdant area carpeted with lush grass and surrounded by beds of tropical plants and flowers in an array of brilliant colors. Quite a contrast to the February drab Oklahoma City was wearing right now. The lawn extended out some seventy-five yards where it met a waist-high, white stucco fence. Beyond the fence she could see the cloud-shrouded Andes. "Your home is lovely," she said.

He looked up from his coffee. "Thank you. It suits my needs."

Well, I should hope so, Alex thought, picturing her unpretentious house with only half the space and a third the acreage of this rambling hilltop residence. Yet Vicente lived here alone, surrounded by comfort and all the trappings of wealth.

Her family home, even though large and roomy, in no way equalled this. The Harpers were upper middle class, with a weekly cleaning woman and a landscape service for the lawn. Well-off, but hardly in the same league as Vicente and Juan Carlos, who employed a regular staff here at Casa Serrano and probably many more at their country home. It must be nice, Alex mused, to take such luxury for granted. But there was no point in comparing their life-styles.

Actually his affluence could work to her advantage. She was in a strange country, trying to track an elusive celebrity, the only things in her favor, a command of Spanish and some knowledge of the author, based on letters and books. She'd need any help she could get to locate Camila, and Vicente's status in the community might be an asset.

Vicente glanced at his watch. "We must leave soon if we're going to beat the crowds to the market."

"We?" Alex felt irritation rising within her. How much longer did he intend to escort her around? She was beginning to wonder about his motives for putting himself out to entertain her. Opening up his home was enough. Why the extra attention?

"Really, Señor Serrano. I'm a big girl, quite capable of making my own way without inconveniencing others." She rose from the table and turned toward the servant. "Luisa, would you please summon a taxi for me? I'll stop by my suite for a moment, then be right down." With no argument coming from Vicente, Alex went upstairs to brush her teeth and grab her purse and a notebook, pleased with herself for using the direct approach so successfully. Within ten minutes she was back in the entry hall on her way outside.

"This isn't a taxi!" When Alex reached the doorstep, Vicente was opening the door of an Isuzu Trooper, which he obviously planned to use for chauffeuring her around.

"Sorry, but it was too late to have a meter installed," he said sarcastically. "You can pay for the gasoline if you insist, or just give me a generous gratuity when we get there."

Alex raised her hands in defeat. Apparently the man was determined to stick with her, and she didn't have time to argue. Vicente wasn't the only one who'd suggested getting to Otavalo early. So had the guidebook.

"How long is the drive?" she asked as she buckled her seat belt.

"About an hour and a half. Just relax and enjoy the scenery along the way." His words and tone were cordial, yet Alex sensed a tenseness in his manner. She'd first noticed it when she'd mentioned Camila last night. But Camila hadn't entered the conversation this morning. So what was going on? She couldn't put her finger on it—the slight frown or the coolness in his eyes—but she didn't think she was imagining the undercurrent.

But if he felt she was imposing, why had he taken on the role of the perfect host? After all, he'd insisted she stay with him, and then offered to drive her around. Could it be that he didn't have a choice? Did Vicente feel obliged to be more accommodating than he really wanted to be?

Perhaps he was just following instructions from his father. Parents exercised a lot more control here than in the States, even over adult children.

Now Alex wondered about the phone conversation he'd been having when she'd appeared on the patio. A girlfriend, obviously. Possibly a significant someone he'd hoped to spend Saturday with.

Vicente was definitely the sort of man who would never be without a woman in his life. He knew just what to say and do—and yet except for that telephone call, there was no evidence of a special woman.

Discreetly she studied him as he maneuvered the Trooper through the curvy mountainous route out of the city. He was a confident driver, taking the busy traffic in stride, one hand skillfully steering, while the other rested on the gear shift.

Last night he'd been dressed in a dark suit with a white shirt and paisley tie. Now he was far more informal, wearing casual maroon slacks and matching knit pullover, but he was no less immaculate. Dark hair feathered his forearms, and despite the sunglasses he wore, Alex could see that his thick black brows were scrunched together in a half frown. Was he troubled or simply deep in thought?

"Do you think it might be possible to run into someone who knows Camila?" she asked, trying to sound matter-of-fact.

He shrugged, then gave her a sideways glance. "There will be time enough later to talk about Camila. Better first to get a sense of the country and background information for your article."

Alex started to argue that she didn't have that much time and also that she didn't need help in formulating what she should do, but decided to appear compliant for the moment. For some reason Vicente Serrano was opposed to her search for Camila, and eventually she'd figure out why.

"I'm sorry to be pestering you with my comments. But, as I've indicated already, it's really not necessary that you escort me everywhere. I'm quite capable of getting around on my own. By car or bus, if necessary."

"Nonsense. Do you honestly think you could get around by bus?" He pointed to one approaching them and chuckled. "Somehow I can't imagine you as part of that scene."

The decrepit old vehicle was crammed with humanity, every square inch of the windows filled with the faces of men, women and children. On top, a few pieces of luggage bumped alongside crates of live chickens and fresh vegetables and bunches of green bananas.

"I could do it if I had to," she said huffily. "But if it'll make you happy, I'll rent a car for future trips."

"You're a child, and a female one at that. It wouldn't be safe driving unknown roads by yourself."

Alex turned in her seat, unable to rein in her temper. "I realize I'm a lot younger than you are, but hardly a child, and I assure you I can take care of myself."

A stalled truck was blocking the roadway and Vicente brought the car to a halt. He turned to her and silently his eyes examined her body, his survey beginning with the knees showing at the hem of her split skirt, moving up to her waist, pausing at her small breasts, then meeting her eyes. "Forgive me," he said, his voice low. "You're most definitely a woman, and yes, much younger than I. But then thirty-four is not so old, hmm?"

His perusal and the veiled suggestiveness in his voice caused Alex to shiver. She wished she'd held her tongue. He'd quickly and seductively twisted her comment about being able to take care of herself, and now she was questioning her own words. Could she really take care of herself with Vicente Serrano around? Somehow she doubted it, especially if he decided to shower her with charm. For a moment she'd been certain he contemplated kissing her, possibly to teach her a lesson for remarking on their age difference. Alex almost sighed with relief when the road was finally cleared and Vicente turned his attention back to driving.

Before long the car veered off the highway and onto a side road leading into the town of Otavalo. "We'll park here," he told her, finding a space on one of the narrow streets. "You'll probably want to do some shopping."

"Why do men assume all women are interested in shopping?" Alex objected. "I can do that in the mall back home."

When Vicente came around to open her door, he was laughing.

"What's so funny?"

"You. Take a look around here and then tell me that it compares to a North American shopping center."

Alex got out of the car, slamming the door loudly in response to his laughter and desperately trying to think of a snappy comeback to his condescending remark. But nothing came to mind, and she sulkily went along as they made their way to the heart of the market. Within minutes they reached a square thronged with people, all buying or selling or socializing. The bustling activities of the market soon made Alex forget her irritation with Vicente.

The Indians were dressed in their native garb—the men in navy ponchos and dark snap brims and the women in intricately embroidered white peasant blouses with multiple strands of gold-colored beads around their necks. Some of the women carried babies papoose-style. "Those are the Otavaleños," Vicente told her. "You can recognize them by their distinctive clothes."

Alex noticed how all the men wore stark-white pants and had a single black braid trailing down their backs. Judging from the length of the braids, their hair had never been cut.

Along with the natives buying foodstuffs, tourists were converging on the marketplace. Alex felt an infusion of optimism. Maybe she could accomplish something today—absorb some local color, get a feel for the people and, despite her shopping disclaimer, purchase a few souvenirs for her family.

The panorama before her was inspiring. Finding Camila might be a long shot, but for the first time Alex felt confident she could put together a credible article for *Newsmakers*. And her dissertation would be greatly improved by these personal experiences. She pulled out a pad and pen from her purse and jotted down a couple of notes before succumbing to the lure of the market again.

Alex was fascinated by the goods. By the time she and Vicente had threaded their way past all the displays and booths, she'd managed to buy colorful wool sweaters for her sisters, a straw sun hat for her mother, a tapestry for her father's office and a patio dress for herself.

Twice she'd attempted to ask about Camila, quizzing two merchants as to whether they'd seen the writer at the market. Both times, Vicente had pulled her away to show her something of interest. First a litter of puppies, then a whole roasted pig with long red chilies jutting from its ears and a lemon in its mouth. Alex found these interruptions extremely disconcerting. It was almost as if he was deliberately trying to distract her from the subject of Camila.

"I guess I should be grateful you didn't want to shop." Vicente was at her side, laden down with her purchases. "Otherwise I wouldn't be able to see over this stack to find my way back to the car." He arched one dark brow at her.

"Shopping was your idea," she said. "Don't blame me if I took your advice to heart."

They passed a house with a red-flowered tree, its huge blooms hanging over the wall. "The flowers on that tree look like poinsettias," she said, taking out her camera.

"That's because they are, but here we call them *flor de Panama.*"

"They're amazing." She thought of the small Christmas plants back home. They paled in comparison to these beauties. She turned back toward the square, snapping several more pictures, then dropped the camera into her bag. "Okay, let's go."

"It's almost twelve. Where to now?"

"How about Hostería Chorlaví for lunch?" she suggested, surprised he was letting her make a decision for a change. "The guidebook says it's a local favorite." It was also a favorite of Camila's, another special place she'd remarked upon in her letters, but there was no point in bringing that up with Vicente.

The hacienda-style restaurant contained a two-story patio for dining. The morning chill had left the air, leaving the temperature perfect for an outside meal. Both Vicente and Alex had worked up an appetite, and they ate heartily. First soup, then chicken with lemons and *ají*—a yellow salsa of tomatoes, scallions, chilies and cilantro. They lingered at their corner table while nearby a band played festive music that enticed diners into putting down their forks and knives and clapping along.

Although she'd grumbled about Vicente accompanying her and wasn't even one step closer to Camila, Alex realized she was gathering valuable insight into the country, and she couldn't help but enjoy herself. The day had been an excursion into a whole new world.

Vicente poured a cup of hot tea for each of them. "Would you consider letting me read your dissertation?" he asked. "That is, if you brought it to Ecuador with you."

His request surprised her. "I brought it, and I suppose you can read it, although I'm not sure I understand the reason for your interest."

He shrugged. "Curiosity, I guess. I'm still wondering about the real reason you're investigating an obscure South American writer. Not to mention why your interest seems to be more than professional." His expression was intense—and like last night—conveyed a certain distrust.

Alex was startled by the bluntness of Vicente's comments. "Well," she said, "I would disagree with the 'obscure' bit. Perhaps, as you said, she's not as well-known as some, but she's becoming quite a name in the United States. And I thought we'd already discussed what she means to me."

"Indulge me," he said.

"To begin with, as a literature major, I appreciate her talent for writing. As a woman, I like her approach to life, the complex mixture of fearlessness and femininity in her books. She's a role model—someone I can relate to."

"Behold," he said, "a sexist. You like what she's done because she's a female."

"Yes . . . no. That's not what I meant. You're twisting my words."

Vicente chuckled. "Don't be embarrassed. We're all guilty of sexism at times."

"I am not a sexist."

"If you say so." His tone was one of amusement, which only aggravated Alex.

"Should we leave now?" she asked, noticing several people waiting for tables.

Vicente agreed, and they both rose and walked toward the lobby to pay the bill.

As the cashier took Vicente's credit card, the proprietor approached Alex. "Did you enjoy your meal?"

"It was wonderful," she said. "I understand your restaurant is a favorite of Camila Zavala's, too."

"Really? I'm pleased to hear it, but surprised, as well. I was never aware that she was here."

Alex paused. "Well, perhaps she didn't identify herself. She seems to savor her privacy."

"That is true."

Just then a hand took her arm, and Vicente said curtly, "It's time to go."

"Surely we're not in that big a rush—"

"Oh, but we are. There are several other places I want to show you today. Besides, Señor Morales needs to return to his patrons." He shook hands with the owner, bidding him farewell, then nudged Alex toward the door.

Alex had half a mind to do a little nudging herself—such as an elbow to his ribs. She really didn't believe that showing her the sights was all that important to Vicente. She got in the car and stared out the window, refusing to make eye contact with him.

Obviously aware she was perturbed, Vicente let out
a sigh of resignation. "Okay, so I admit to hurrying
you a little."

"A little?" Alex shook her head in amazement.
"Maybe it's time for me to make it perfectly clear that
I'm not here for enjoyment and I don't have to be
carted around like visiting royalty, nor do I have to be
told where to go and when. I don't like being hustled
out of restaurants as if I pose a health risk."

"You're exaggerating. Besides, you were the one
who suggested we leave. I was only trying to ensure
that you visited the places you want to see."

Sure, Alex thought. "Well, your methods leave
something to be desired."

"Then I apologize for my methods. Now, why don't
we try to get back to enjoying this damn trip."

In spite of her anger, Alex couldn't help but smile
at his clenched teeth. Good. He was irritated. Served
him right.

They drove to Cotacachi, famous for its leather
products, then visited Cuicocha Lake, a national park.
During most of the trip, they were silent except for
Vicente's occasional brief comments about sights.
Alex just wished she had a clue to the thoughts going
on behind those veiled eyes of his. "I don't know
what's really bothering you," she finally said, "but if
you're not happy with your role as tour guide, then
stop being one."

"Happiness has nothing to do with it," he assured
her. "If I appear to have something bothering me, it's

probably because it's been a long day. We'll head back to Quito now."

Just like a man, Alex mused. We eat when they're hungry and go home when they're ready. If she hadn't been so relieved at the prospect of escaping his company, she would have demanded he take her somewhere else. But it *had* been a long day, and she needed to organize her thoughts before deciding what to do next, so she shifted her gaze back to the side window, concentrating on the scenery rather than him.

To avoid construction, they detoured onto a road that ran alongside a stream. A woman sat on the bank nursing a baby. Other women were washing laundry in the water, beating the clothes against rocks. Farther on, a sow and her piglets rooted at the side of the road, unperturbed by the traffic. Finally Vicente rejoined the main route. The contrast between the side road and the highway had been a good diversion for Alex, since it took her mind off her companion.

But that only lasted until they arrived back at Casa Serrano. There she found herself annoyed all over again. "Thank you for showing me around," she said formally as she started into the house. "But as I explained, from now on I'll do my exploring alone and—"

"Let's go in here. The hallway has no privacy." He pulled her into a nearby room and closed the door. The phone rang just as they stepped inside.

"*Sí,*" he said impatiently into the intercom. "I'll take the call."

He gestured for her to sit, but she remained standing as he wrestled with a seemingly urgent business problem.

Obviously this was Vicente's study. She noted that the walls were decorated with plaques and a number of photographs of Vicente and his father. It was an impressive display—a citation from the mayor for civic activities, a picture taken with two U.S. senators, another with a famous Hollywood movie star, awards from the Red Cross and several philanthropic organizations. Apparently the Serrano influence and contacts were widespread.

Vicente hung up the phone. "Now, what were we discussing?"

"I was telling you that I prefer to make my own arrangements while I'm in Ecuador. I don't wish to interfere with your schedule any more than I already have."

"*¡Vaya!* Forget my schedule. That is trivial. What concerns me is that you've no sense of what you're getting into. Don't you realize this pursuit of Camila Zavala could cause problems?"

"For whom?"

"For yourself."

"Problems such as . . . ?"

"Such as putting yourself in a dangerous situation."

"That's absurd." Alex knew something that Vicente didn't. Although there had been rumors of threats, according to Camila's last letter, they had been

a public relations ploy by her publisher. "Sure Camila has stepped on a few toes," said Alex. "But that
can't automatically be equated with danger."

"You never know." Vicente's brow furrowed.
"There are unscrupulous individuals who'd like
nothing better than to silence Camila, especially since
she's writing about exploitation of the Amazon's natural resources."

"Does that include you, Señor Serrano? After all,
oil is a natural resource and it's your business."

"And your father's business, too. You have to agree
that the industry has plenty of honorable people,
many as concerned about the habitat as the environ-
mentalists."

He moved toward the wall to single out one of the
plaques. "And that includes our company. This
award, for example. Forgive me if I seem to lack hu-
mility, but I point it out to you as proof of what I'm
saying. We have several initiatives to ensure that ex-
ploration is not synonymous with exploitation."

Alex walked over to read the inscription. It was a
recognition of the Serranos' efforts from an international wildlife organization. "Very impressive," she
said.

"Thank you. But we were discussing the potential
danger—"

"Pure speculation. If you're attempting to make me
leave with scare tactics, it won't work."

"You are very obstinate." He grabbed her by the
arms and pulled her close, their faces only inches

apart. "If I wanted to get rid of you, why did I ask you to stay here in the first place?"

That was the same question she'd been posing to herself, and as ridiculous as it seemed, she thought she knew the answer. "So you can keep an eye on me, maybe even prevent me from finding Camila."

Vicente smiled. "I must say I enjoy keeping my eye on you. But what is my reason for keeping you from Camila?"

"I don't know," she admitted.

He shook his head ruefully. "All I've tried to do is advise you, to help you understand. Searching for someone who wants anonymity is unwise, *querida*."

The endearment caught Alex completely off guard and appeared to surprise Vicente, too. Their gaze held and for a moment she once again thought that he was about to kiss her. Instead, his hold loosened, and he walked over to his desk. "It's late and I have calls to return." His voice was steady, the tone a clear dismissal.

Alex retreated to the safety of her room, telling herself she was glad to be free of him. But she couldn't explain why her pulse was still unsteady. She didn't understand what was happening to her, why she felt so unsettled. She didn't even *like* Vicente Serrano. He was confusing, controlling—and probably too old for her. Worse, he was obviously concealing information about Camila. Information she needed. Still, there was something about Vicente that drew her to him, and Alex was honest enough to admit that the attraction had nothing to do with Camila.

CHAPTER THREE

ALEX HAD JUST REMOVED her shoes and begun un-
dressing in preparation for a bath when a knock
sounded on her bedroom door. Pausing to rebutton
her blouse, she walked over to the door and opened it.

Vicente stood on the threshold, not attempting to
enter. "I'm very sorry. I forgot to mention that Luisa
will bring a tray of food whenever you're hungry.
There's a buzzer on your wall to signal her." His words
were matter-of-fact, those of a considerate host seeing to the needs of a guest.

Why then, Alex wondered, were her thoughts
straying from the mundane to the erotic? The man had
suggested nothing more personal than a meal. Yet her
body experienced a slight tingle, responding as though
she was back in Vicente's arms again. She glanced up
at him, hoping he wouldn't notice the telltale blush she
could feel coloring her cheeks. His ill temper seemed
to have vanished completely and his eyes held a soft
warmth. This Vicente Serrano was definitely harder to
dislike, harder to resist.

"Thank you for telling me," she finally said, draw-
ing herself back to reality. She had to admit she'd been
touched by his attentions during the day. Even when

disagreeable, he had managed to be appealing. Later she would examine the stirrings he'd aroused in her— much later. Because she felt certain her emotions were likely to remain sensitized for a long time.

"I will see you in the morning, then. I regret I cannot join you for a meal tonight, but there are some deadlines I have to meet."

Alex shut the door and crossed to the bed. As she dropped onto the side of the mattress, a tiny voice advised her to pack her bags and leave before her attraction to Vicente Serrano got in the way of her work. She needed to focus on her goal. In just a few weeks she had to come up with a credible article about Camila Zavala, and Vicente had made it clear that he'd give her no assistance. So why was she staying here, allowing him to distract her?

Because you're being practical. Vicente knows more about Camila Zavala than he's letting on. By just biding your time, maybe you'll figure out how to maneuver him into helping you.

Alex touched her fingertips to her lips, the action belying her pretense of calm objectivity. With a plaintive sigh, she got to her feet and went into the adjoining bathroom to fill the tub. A long soak would not only wash away the grit of the day, but perhaps soothe her troubled soul.

An hour or so later, bathed and pleasantly satiated by the meal Luisa had brought, she reached for her journal to make notes of the day's events. Fortunately she was able to lose herself in the task and hours passed as she worked, stopping only when her shoulders began to ache. Time to quit. Alex pulled off her glasses and began preparing for bed.

The night was quiet, and she could hear sounds from Vicente's suite next door, the gurgling pipes telling her that he, too, must have been working and was now taking a late-night shower. Lying in bed, Alex couldn't prevent herself from picturing Vicente showering, the water sluicing down his bare torso....

She was supposed to be concentrating on Camila, not Vicente Serrano. Fantasizing about men was alien to Alex. Still, she kept thinking about Vicente's lips close to hers. Why hadn't he kissed her? Surely she wasn't imagining that he'd wanted to. And for some ridiculous reason, she was disappointed he'd changed his mind. Why was she even entertaining such thoughts of kisses and the complications that went with them?

Too many *whys* and too few answers. She had to stop muddling her mind with all this foolishness. Vicente didn't want a fling with her, nor she with him. She was in Ecuador for only a short while, and a romantic interlude didn't fit into her plans. Yet her mind refused to cooperate by staying away from the subject of Vicente. It was hours before she finally drifted off to sleep.

The sun peeking through the draperies awakened Alex the next morning. She pulled the covers over her head and snuggled deeper into the warmth of the bed. It couldn't be dawn already—she'd only just closed her eyes! But a quick peek at her watch confirmed that it was slightly after six.

She recalled Vicente's telling her how the days were always the same length in Quito—sunrise around six a.m. and sunset around six p.m. Interesting and different from what she was used to, but not very welcome at the moment. Especially for Alex, who'd always had difficulty sleeping in the daylight. Reluctantly she threw the blankets aside and headed for the bathroom. With a full day at her computer planned, she might as well get started.

Vicente was nowhere around when she came down for a quick breakfast. Luisa explained that he'd left early, with instructions for Alex to ask for whatever she needed.

As it turned out, Alex's needs were few. She had set up her laptop computer in the private study Vicente had told her to use. Pulling out her scribbled notes, she started working.

She took a break at one for lunch and then another in the late afternoon for a walk around the estate. When she decided to stop for the day, a light supper awaited in the dining room, and Vicente joined her for the meal. He apologized for his earlier absence and said that he would be unavailable again this evening. As soon as they'd eaten, he disappeared into his study.

IF SHE'D THOUGHT Vicente had abandoned the solicitous-host routine, Alex soon realized her mistake.

"Unfortunately I have several appointments today, so I'll be tied up again," Vicente explained over breakfast the next morning. "However, I've arranged for a colleague, Pablo Rodríguez, to drive you to Calderón."

"That's really not necessary," Alex objected. "I'm not interested in an escort. Forgive my directness, but you're stifling me by being overprotective."

He reached over to take her hand, rekindling memories of Saturday. She jerked the hand away and he smiled, his dimples deepening.

"I don't want you to feel stifled, Alex, but allow me to do this. I would worry if you were traveling outside the city alone. Permit me to look out for you."

His smile may have been the most devastating in South America, but Alex wasn't going to let any momentary vulnerability destroy her common sense, which told her that, despite his posture of concern, Vicente Serrano simply didn't want her striking off on her own. Her blue eyes took on a frosty hue. "I don't need your hired hand trailing around after me and interfering in my business," she said.

Vicente laughed. "Pablo's hardly a hired hand, and I give you my word he will not interfere. He'll simply be along to serve as your driver and guide. Not only is he a trusted associate, but also a good friend, and most women find him quite entertaining. Perhaps you will enjoy yourself, hmm?"

He smiled again and Alex's objections faded. Why be difficult? She'd told Vicente at dinner yesterday that she wanted to go to the town of Calderón. It would be much easier for her to accept the offer of a ride than to spend half the morning arranging transportation. At least Vicente himself wasn't coming along to look over her shoulder, and maybe this Pablo character wouldn't be so closemouthed when it came to providing some insight into Camila's whereabouts.

Like the market in Otavalo, the Christmas-ornament workshop in Calderón was a gamble, but it was on a carefully compiled list of locations frequented by Camila, places mentioned in her novels and letters. Camila had apparently been there at least once, because Alex had received a box of the handmade ornaments from her one Christmas. As it stood now, Alex had few clues, so she had to investigate every possibility.

Alex smiled back at Vicente, nodding her acquiescence. If he wanted to furnish her with a chauffeur, then she'd let him.

Pablo Rodríguez was an amiable man with regular features and the same gracious Ecuadoran manners she'd seen repeatedly the past few days. He seemed fairly benign, chatting agreeably as he shifted the gears of his green Volvo to negotiate the curves on the road to Calderón. But Alex knew the truth—he would report back to Vicente everything that happened.

Nevertheless, the drive was enjoyable, lasting little more than thirty minutes and giving Alex another view of the countryside. The workshop, which Alex had expected to be bustling with creative activity, was actually a small warehouse and showroom. Pablo explained that the ornaments were made in the various artisans' homes and brought there for distribution.

Alex was pleasantly surprised to discover that the owners of the Christmas Connection, Alan and Debbie Sutton, were originally from Texas. Perhaps the couple would be more forthcoming with a fellow North American than her host had been.

Alan and Debbie had arrived in Quito some ten years earlier, both on Fulbright grants. When their grants expired, they'd married and taken teaching positions so they could remain in the country. To Alex's eyes they seemed like throwbacks to the idealistic, simple-living hippies of the sixties. Debbie had a full mane of wavy auburn hair, and Alan sported a long beard. Both wore jeans and boots and Western shirts. But Alex soon realized they were also savvy entrepreneurs. Their dream of an import-export company, which had taken root in the early days of their stay in Ecuador, had come to fruition, and they now employed more than a hundred people.

"The heart of the business is the Christmas stuff, but we export all types of merchandise—textiles, jewelry, leathers," Debbie Sutton told Alex as they studied the shelves of articles.

"Christmas is my favorite holiday," Alex said excitedly, picking up a shopping basket and selecting an array of ornaments to take home. "These'll make great gifts for my friends." As Debbie wrapped the purchases in newspaper, they chatted about the differences between North and South America and about Alex's visit. As briefly as she could, Alex laid out the purpose of her trip, including her objective of interviewing Camila Zavala. "Do you know her?"

Debbie smiled. "Of course. Everyone in Ecuador knows of Camila. She's a national treasure."

"Then you've met her?" Alex asked hopefully.

"Unfortunately, no," Debbie said, quickly extinguishing the moment of optimism. "At least not that we know of," she continued, "since her real identity is a secret."

"As I'm sure you've considered, Camila Zavala is probably a pseudonym," Alan added. "But we'd certainly like to meet her, whoever she is. She must be a fascinating person."

At the mention of Camila, Alex noticed a flicker of interest in Pablo's dark eyes as he looked up from the tray of ornaments he was fingering. Although she hadn't quizzed him on the ride up, she definitely would later. For now, though, she needed to concentrate on the Suttons. "But she mentioned your workshop in one of her books."

"Oh, yes." Debbie smiled. "We were thrilled. The business was just getting started and the plug gave it a boost. Apparently Camila does that a lot—lends her name to causes, donates money to needy groups, even gives a hand to struggling new businesses. I wish there were some way to say thanks, but that seems unlikely. If we've ever met her, we weren't aware of it. We have many women customers. She could be any one of the ladies who comes in."

"Then you've no idea how I could find her?"

Alan laughed. "All I can say is lots of luck. From what I've heard, you'd have stood a better chance of interviewing Garbo in her lifetime than of getting to Camila."

"That bad, huh?" Alex chewed on the tip of her sunglasses.

"Probably worse. I hate to throw cold water on your plans, but I suggest you forget the notion of a meeting. Even if you succeeded, it could result in trouble."

"Like what?"

Alan cleared his throat. "You know. From those who object to things she's written."

"You make her sound like Salman Rushdie. Camila's works are probing, but not nearly so incendiary." Alex brushed her hair back off her face.

"We're not trying to be alarmists, Alex, but you have to remember that this is a different society than what you're used to."

"And I'm not trying to be difficult," Alex said. "But I keep being told that trying to write this article is dangerous. However, I need more concrete reasons to believe that. So far it's just been rumors and intimation."

"Surely you read the news accounts of the problems after her previous book was released. *Death of the Amazon* is even more of an indictment against crooked businessmen than that one was," Debbie said.

"I happen to know that those were part of her publisher's attempts to increase sales. Have you seen anything to indicate otherwise?"

"No," answered Debbie.

"Neither have I," Alan admitted. "I suppose we're just being protective. There's always the threat of media exposure causing problems—Camila's effectiveness might be permanently damaged if her identity was discovered. I'm sure you wouldn't want that on your conscience."

"Of course not. But I only want to meet Camila, not expose her."

Alan leaned against the counter. "We're not saying you would. But it might be out of your control."

"Thanks for the advice," Alex said with as much false enthusiasm as she could muster. The Suttons obviously had good intentions, but she wished she could find someone, *anyone*, who would offer help, instead of unwanted admonishments to forget Camila. Nevertheless, she smiled warmly and tucked the package of ornaments into the large leather tote she'd bought in Cotacachi.

"Please visit us again if you're up this way," Debbie said as the couple walked Alex and Pablo to the door. "And say hello to Vicente."

Alex was taken aback. "You know Vicente?"

"Oh, my, yes," Debbie answered. "He's a friend. When we started out, we had little money, but lots of ideas and energy. Vicente eased the way for a substantial bank loan. It was through his help we were able to grow so large. Vicente realized that our increased business would mean more jobs for the people here in Calderón. He's a wonderful man, very honorable and totally committed to his country."

Alex was amazed by this information. The description of Vicente as honorable seemed particularly incongruous to her, especially considering that he knew the Suttons but had omitted telling her so. Had he thought it would affect her decision to come? She also had to wonder if he'd provided the pair a script of what to say when she arrived. They seemed to be reciting the same lines as Vicente. After all, they were beholden to him.

"For now, *chau,*" Alan said.

"Chau," Alex replied, echoing his goodbye and thinking how it sounded more Italian than Spanish. She shook hands with both of them, then she and Pablo made their way back to the car.

"I hope you weren't too bored while I was talking to the Suttons." She smiled at Pablo as they drove away from the factory.

"Not at all. They're nice people. And I know Vicente thinks highly of them."

"Unfortunately they couldn't give me much assistance in my search for Camila Zavala." Trying to appear casual, she added, "Do you have any idea how I could go about locating her?"

Was it her imagination or did Pablo's mouth tighten slightly? "She's not easy to find."

"So everyone says. But that doesn't really answer my question. Have you met her? Do you know her real name?"

Pablo paused. "Allow me to offer you a caveat..."

Oh great, she thought, more warnings about looking for Camila. And sure enough, Pablo explained the folly of continuing on what he called a "quixotic" search for the writer. Obviously Vicente and his friends overestimated the problem while underestimating her tenacity. They seemed almost paranoid about protecting Camila's identity, giving Alex no credit for discretion. She didn't plan on publishing Camila's address and telephone number in *Newsmakers* for heaven's sake!

"Thank you for taking me," she said to Pablo as they arrived at the outskirts of Quito.

"It was my pleasure. Vicente and I have been like brothers since boyhood. I am more than willing to stand in for him, especially with such a charming *señorita.*"

Vicente came out the front door as soon as the car stopped. Alex presumed he was there to greet his friend and see them both inside and was therefore bemused by his rather abrupt dismissal of Pablo. "I don't want to keep you longer, *amigo mío,*" he said before the other man had a chance to get out of his car. "We'll see you in a few days."

"Thank you again for escorting me," Alex called, doubting that she would see Pablo again, despite Vicente's use of "we." She needed to get on with her work—she'd been in Ecuador almost seventy-two hours and thus far hadn't accomplished anything of substance. Worse, she hadn't figured out how to go about finding out anything more. Heading for the university library was one possibility. Unfortunately, though, Alex knew that finding Camila there was highly unlikely.

Nevertheless, she passed the next two days at the Universidad Católica Biblioteca. The first morning was frustrating. She had the opportunity to question several personnel about the author, but no one was very helpful, leaving Alex to wonder whether Vicente Serrano's influence extended to the library staff.

She decided to go directly to the literature department. Perhaps there she'd find someone willing to provide guidance, maybe even take her back to the library. The staff might be more accommodating to one of their own.

Even with Alex's fluency in Spanish, locating the right office and the right person was a challenge. It was late afternoon before she met Profesora Belén Espinoza, who was also a fan of Camila and apparently one of the few people not coached by Vicente. There was instant camaraderie, since the woman's enthusiasm was almost as great as Alex's.

They chatted for an hour, then made an appointment to meet at the library the next morning, Belén promising to show Alex where to find the material concerning Camila.

The second day was well spent. The stacks contained several magazine and newspaper articles Alex hadn't seen before. That in itself was useful, but the real plum was the discovery of an unfamiliar novel—actually, Camila's first—*Andes Images*. It appeared to have been published by a now defunct company and hadn't been translated into English or circulated outside of Ecuador. Whether Alex managed to locate Camila or not, the trip had more than paid off thanks to this find.

An obscure work, the perfect hook for an article. The only problem was that this edition could not be checked out, and it appeared to be long out of print. But perhaps one of the bookstores in Quito still had a copy. She jotted down the necessary information, then decided to return to Vicente's house to spend the rest of the day calling booksellers.

After a quick lunch, Alex started phoning the names on a list of booksellers she'd compiled from the telephone directory. Much to her consternation, her efforts were totally fruitless. Either the phone wasn't answered or she was left on hold or they didn't want to look.

Choosing to visit the stores in person, Alex explored several modern ones along Juan Leon Mera. While she bought three books to add to her own library, Alex had no success in finding Camila's first novel. She tucked her purchases into her tote and took a taxi to the historical district. If *Andes Images* was still available, a bookstore there might have a copy. She got out of the cab near a colonial church that was undergoing renovations. Ducking beneath the scaffolding, she stepped inside to view the work. Despite its state of upheaval, the sanctuary glowed with a wondrous antiquity. She longed to linger, but one glance at her watch and she hurried back outside. It was after four now, and she wanted to get to the two nearest shops before they closed.

She was only steps from the church when several men, women and children crowded around her, jostling her as she walked. For some reason, Alex felt threatened, immediately sensing that this was not a friendly group. The pushing was too aggressive for an ordinary sidewalk crush and twice she felt a tugging at her leather tote. She was about to call for help when a hand closed around her wrist.

"You little fool!"

Alex looked up into the angry face of Vicente Serrano.

"I told you you were taking ridiculous chances," he barked, his dark eyes flashing.

"Not really," Alex countered as she leaned into the safety of Vicente's arms. She couldn't stifle a shiver as she glanced around, checking up and down the street. The group had scattered at Vicente's approach. "No, all you gave me were vague warnings about some mysterious danger."

"Warnings you ignored." He ran his hands over her body, causing her fear to evaporate and another, more intimate, sensation to take its place.

"What are you searching for? Bullet wounds?" she growled, embarrassed by her reaction to his touch.

"How about stab wounds?" He shoved his hand through a slit in her leather bag. The thick hide was cut clean through, even the bag's lining severed. "Is anything missing?"

Alex loosened the drawstring handle and rummaged through the bag, sighing with relief upon locating her wallet, traveler's checks and passport. "Nothing important. How did you happen to be here?"

"Pure chance. I'd just left a business meeting when I saw you."

She shivered again. "Thank you for rescuing me."

Vicente glanced around. "They could return. Come. My car's on the next block. Let's get out of here before you land in any more trouble."

Alex was too shaken to argue.

The ride back to Vicente's home was silent, and Alex was grateful that he was no longer chastising her.

The respite from his sharp tongue lasted, however, only until he'd pulled into the drive. Once he'd turned off the engine, he shifted his body to look at her, leaning on the steering wheel. "Now will you recognize the danger in searching for Camila?"

Alex laughed harshly. "I can't believe this! Those people didn't know I was looking for Camila." Once she'd had some time to recover, Alex could view the incident rationally. "It was nothing more than a simple mugging. Something that happens in big cities all over the world. I'm obviously a tourist—" she tugged on a strand of her golden hair "—and they planned to grab a few dollars. It was frightening but it wasn't some international terrorist ring trying to murder me."

"How can you be certain?"

"There are few certainties in life, but tell me, do you honestly think I'm in danger? Should I arrange for a bodyguard?"

"I think this conversation has become tiresome." He opened the door and got out of the car.

Alex smiled. He'd all but admitted there was no danger. His warnings had been a ruse to discourage her search for Camila. "The bookstores," she said as Vicente was opening the car door for her.

"What?"

"I went to the historical district to check out some bookstores. I'll have to return tomorrow."

Vicente looked incredulous.

Animatedly she told him of the obscure Zavala novel she'd found. "It's not the same as an interview, but it's a good place to start the article. I need to find a copy."

The expression on Vicente's face seemed to say he wished she'd forget about Camila, but his words were placating. "We'll go out for dinner and talk about locating it, then." He reached down and broke off a rose from a bush near the driveway, handing it to her. It wasn't necessarily meant to be a romantic gesture, but Alex experienced a tiny flutter in her chest. At times like this, it was difficult to remember how much of a pain Vicente often was.

As promised, he took her out to eat, a casual meal at the Hotel Colón coffee shop. Over cups of espresso, he leaned toward her. "Apparently it's become necessary that I be of more help."

"What?" Was Vicente really willing to assist?

"If you'll give me the information on the novel you're looking for, I'll have one of my associates search for it. Maybe we can come up with a copy. Better yet, I mentioned earlier that my father wanted to meet you. He knows many people, some with extensive personal libraries. Perhaps if you talked with him, you could persuade him to make some calls. We could visit the hacienda tomorrow—it's not a long distance away—and return to Quito Friday."

Now he was even offering his father's aid. Alex had begun to wonder whether Vicente Serrano was more saboteur than supporter, so this offer left her downright skeptical. But the best course seemed to be seeing it through. She wasn't enthusiastic about rummaging through anymore bookstores on her own. Especially after today's incident. Vicente was much more likely to locate *Andes Images* than she.

Besides, she should probably pay a courtesy call on his father to say thank you for the Serrano hospitality. Since Juan Carlos was retired, he was probably in need of company. Her father would be pleased if she made an effort to meet the older man. "Visiting your father would be wonderful," she said, her feelings more guarded than her words. Was she allowing herself to be manipulated because of some foolish attraction to Vicente Serrano? Alex ignored her nagging conscience and returned to drinking her espresso.

"Now I must ask your indulgence," Vicente said. "There is work to be attended to tonight so I can get away."

"Of course," Alex said. "I'll just use the time to put my notes in order."

HOURS LATER, Alex stood by the chest of drawers in her bedroom and sniffed the rose now resting in a bud vase, thinking about Vicente. He'd been giving her space the past few evenings, going out for business meetings, then coming back only to closet himself in his study. The man appeared consumed by work. Or was he?

She suspected it wasn't all business, but a girlfriend—the one named Silvia. She had phoned twice during his absence and Alex could tell from Luisa's side of the conversations that the housekeeper was being interrogated. Apparently Silvia was very interested in Vicente and his whereabouts.

She remembered how he'd been at supper tonight—unusually handsome in his red silk shirt, his dark eyes twinkling when the conversation took an amusing turn. He had an infectious laugh and impeccable manners, and was always solicitous toward her.

In another time and another place, he would be a serious candidate for Mr. Right. But not for her. She reminded herself that the two of them were quite different. After a few months, with their dissimilar backgrounds and interests, they'd surely tire of one another.

Alex's tastes in men had always run to the academic types—bookish men who shared her fascination with literature. She'd found businessmen too materialistic and superficial, the lone exception being her own father, who loved books as much as she.

By noon the next day, Vicente and Alex were driving south on the Pan-American Highway toward his family's hacienda. Alex was amazed that the major artery was mostly a narrow, two-lane route, not the busy turnpike she'd envisioned. They were even forced to stop for half an hour to accommodate a herd of cattle shuffling slowly across the road, blissfully unaware of the congestion they were causing.

"Well, we're getting close," Vicente said, as he turned off the highway and drove along what was little more than a track. To the side, a herd of llamas grazed behind a wire fence, looking up nonchalantly at the passing car.

"Llamas!" Alex exclaimed. "They're so cute."

Vicente snorted. "You'll hear conflicting opinions on that score. Many of the people who work with llamas see them as vile, nasty-tempered creatures."

"Oh, how disappointing. But I'd still like a photograph. Do we need to ask the owner?"

"You just did." Vicente gave her a quick smile. "This herd belongs to us. You're now on Serrano land. After we settle in and visit with my father, we can walk back here for a closer look. Then you can get your photograph."

They made another turn, the tires bumping over a cattle guard, and Alex could see the Serrano home at the end of a tree-lined drive. "This approach looks like something out of *Gone with the Wind*," she said, enchanted.

The hacienda was a magnificent two-story, whitestone mansion. "It's been in the Serrano family for centuries. My father, grandfather and several other ancestors were born in this house."

"What about you?"

"I was born in Quito. My mother preferred a hospital, so the tradition was broken with me. But that in no way reduces my attachment. This is my home."

Not just one grand residence, but two. Considering his heritage, Vicente lived rather simply in the city—no chauffeur, only a couple of full-time servants. But here, Alex was reminded of the wealth of the Serrano family.

They parked the car in the circular drive near a bubbling fountain, and a butler greeted them on the steps. "Señor, Señorita. The old *señor* is anxiously waiting."

"Have someone show Señorita Harper to her bedroom so she can freshen up. I'll let my father know we've arrived."

Alex followed a maid up a wide stone staircase to a large suite overlooking a flower-filled inner courtyard. The room was airy and spacious and furnished in antiques. One could get quite accustomed to such opulence, she decided. Even though she'd never longed for material things, Alex found it hard to remain unaffected by the lavish surroundings.

Within a few moments, Vicente knocked. "Have I given you enough time?" he asked as she opened the door. She nodded and followed him back downstairs.

"Alexandra!" Halfway across the living room Alex was met by the elder Serrano. The butler's statement about the "old *señor*" was inaccurate. Juan Carlos Serrano might be in his sixties, but he was still much like his son—a suave, sophisticated, handsome man. He placed his hands on Alex's shoulders and kissed her on the cheek in greeting.

"Come, child." Juan Carlos took her arm and led her toward a seating area. He motioned her to a cushioned sofa, then joined her. "Alexandra is as beautiful as you said," he told his son. He gazed at her silently for long moments. "That flaxen hair and the sky blue eyes. She will make some man a lovely bride." He gave Vicente a meaningful glance.

Alex felt her jaw slacken in amazement. But Juan Carlos either didn't see or else chose to ignore the astonishment on her face as he continued, undaunted. "It has been my dearest wish that my son marry. A wish I was beginning to doubt I would live to realize, for he never brings any suitable women to meet his *papi*. Until now."

CHAPTER FOUR

ALEX STRUGGLED for a reply. Darting a look at Vicente, she saw that his skin was flushed—which told her he was as dismayed as she.

"Father," he said, "you are embarrassing our guest."

Juan Carlos smiled apologetically. "Am I? Forgive me, Alexandra." He rose from the sofa and moved toward a nearby bar. "Some champagne, eh, Vicente? To welcome our lovely visitor?"

The next hour passed more smoothly with the three sipping champagne and engaging in polite conversation, Juan Carlos asking after Scott and the other members of Alex's family.

Juan Carlos pointed to a portrait of his late wife, a full-length oil painting that hung over the fireplace. Elena Serrano was dressed in a fiery red gown and black lace mantilla. "She was a beautiful woman, beautiful of face and spirit," Juan Carlos said, his voice tender.

Before he could say anything else, Vicente deftly changed the subject, and Juan Carlos became ebullient as he related the hacienda's history, pointing out other paintings and listening attentively while Alex told him of the places she'd seen in Ecuador. When she mentioned Camila, he didn't react with surprise or displeasure. But he did put her off—diplomatically. "We'll talk of that later. Now, if you'll excuse me, I must rest a bit before dinner. Doctor's orders." He turned to his son.

"Vicente, why don't you show Alexandra the grounds? If you'd like, of course." He glanced at Alex.

"Yes, that sounds fine," she agreed with suspicion. Despite what he'd said, Juan Carlos looked as healthy as a horse and certainly didn't appear to need an afternoon nap. Alex wondered if, like his son, he had some hidden agenda. Still, she didn't want to offend her host. "I've been promised a visit to the llamas," she told him.

Juan Carlos laughed. "Then you'll want to take along your camera. Larry loves to pose." He stood up. "I'll see you at dinner."

"Larry?" she asked Vicente.

"An English friend suggested we name him after Laurence Olivier because he seems to have, ah, thespian qualities."

Alex laughed. "I can't wait to meet this lamoid Olivier."

"I'll introduce you," he promised. "But first, I suggest you get into something more suitable for walking."

As Alex changed into slacks and tennis shoes, she pondered her introduction to Juan Carlos Serrano.

He'd known her purpose for coming to Ecuador was research—so what had motivated his digression into talk of marriage?

It was almost as though a conspiracy was afoot, a plan for everyone she met to discourage or distract her. If Juan Carlos wanted to divert her attention, then he'd succeeded. Despite a pretense of coolheadedness, it had taken Alex the rest of the conversation to regain her equilibrium.

Yet Vicente had seemed equally nonplussed by his father's comments. Either that or he'd displayed superb acting ability. It just didn't add up—unless the elder Serrano was simply indulging himself in a bit of wishful thinking at everyone else's expense.

"Men," she muttered as she tied her hair back with a scarf. They could be terribly confusing sometimes.

The sky was overcast with gunmetal gray clouds as she and Vicente walked down the road toward the pasture housing the small herd of llamas. Several of them munched on grass while others lazed under a tree. An imposing, multicolored male stood by the wire fence watching as they approached. "That's Larry," Vicente said.

Alex extended her hand through the fence and touched the fur on the animal's rump.

"Careful," Vicente warned, pulling her hand back. "These are not household pets. Sometimes they do the unexpected."

"Like what?"

"Maybe nothing more serious than clicking their teeth. But if really irritated, they sometimes spit on you. Larry's famous for that. And rank means nothing to him. Once an important government official got too close and Larry ruined his hand-tailored suit."

"That's hard to believe." Alex patted the llama again. "Good boy. You're as nice as can be," she cooed. The animal responded by blinking serenely at her. "Mind if I take your picture?" She stepped back and took several snaps, with the rest of the herd in the background. The llama seemed to enjoy posing, cocking his head first to one side, then the other, as if trying to get the angle just right for her.

"You charm even the animals," Vicente commented.

"Even?"

His reply was a mere shrug.

A couple of raindrops spattered down. "We'd better return to the house," Vicente said. "You can listen to the rain and relax before dinner."

He left her at the bottom of the stairs. "My father prefers to eat early. Join us in the *sala* around six for a drink."

Alex went to her bedroom. The rumble of thunder told her that the patter of rain was fast becoming a full-fledged storm. She pulled out a notepad, intending to jot down a list of questions about Camila for Juan Carlos, but after writing only a few, she grew drowsy and stretched out on the bed. She dozed for an hour, then roused herself to change for dinner.

She dressed quickly, slipping into a skirt and blouse and high-heeled pumps, then started downstairs, only to pause midway at the sound of Vicente's raised voice. "Is that what you intended when you insisted I invite her to stay at our home?" he asked in Spanish. "When you spoke of it earlier I assumed you were joking. I hardly know the woman. She hardly knows me."

"I was quite serious," Juan Carlos replied, his voice equally loud, his indignation evident. "I ask you to give the matter some thought. You cannot continue the way things are. Please consider my advice on this."

Alex wondered what she should do. It was clearly not the moment to interrupt the Serranos, and she knew she would be guilty of eavesdropping if she remained. But instinct and general nosiness kept her rooted to the spot. After all, they did appear to be talking about her.

"I always consider your advice. But there's no point in debating this particular subject again. We've gone over it repeatedly."

"What can I do to convince you?" Juan Carlos's agitation was clearly increasing. "It is time you settled down. Besides, as I've said, such a marriage will solve all your difficulties, including the problem with Silvia."

"Perhaps I'm not interested in solving that problem. Perhaps I don't need the services of a matchmaker. Perhaps I plan to marry Silvia."

"Do you? That is not the impression I've gotten. There have been ample opportunities over the years if such was your desire. Like you, my son, I am fond of Silvia. But you must admit, as a wife she is unsuitable."

"Other men marry divorcées, Father. You should not hold that against her."

Alex knew she ought to retreat somewhere. Her behavior was incredibly rude, but she felt compelled to stay. Silvia again. She'd thought the two had a close relationship ever since she'd overheard Vicente talking to her so earnestly on the phone. And just last night Alex had come to the conclusion he'd been spending the past few evenings with the woman. Apparently she was close to the truth.

"Divorce is not the only concern, as you well know. She's too unpredictable and controversial, too flamboyant," Juan Carlos went on. "She would interfere with your work. Even without that consideration, Vicente, you surely understand that what is acceptable for other men is not acceptable for a Serrano. You *must* have the blessing of the church."

"This is not the time to wage a futile discussion of our differences on the subject." Vicente's tone held a hint of stubbornness.

"I want an heir." His father's voice was equally determined. "Alexandra is—"

"Enough! This conversation is ludicrous." Vicente's voice softened. "Besides, she will be joining us at any moment."

On hearing his words, Alex tiptoed back up the stairway. In a few minutes, she would come down again, making some noise to signal her impending arrival. She entered her room and stood in front of the mirror rechecking her hair and makeup.

What she'd taken as lighthearted teasing earlier had been much more than that. Apparently Juan Carlos was serious, his hopes and dreams for his son clouding his good judgment. Alex had to agree with Vicente. The idea of a marriage between the two of them was preposterous.

First, as Vicente had said, they barely knew one another. Second, the differences in their cultures created a large chasm—one she doubted she was ready to bridge. She wanted a fulfilling career. Likely Vicente's idea of women's liberation was days of shopping and nights of parties. Their homes, their families, their lives, were literally and figuratively miles apart.

She glanced nervously at her watch. Only a couple of minutes had passed. Why did she feel so flustered and foolish? Acting as though being Vicente's bride was even a possibility. She'd given little thought to marriage before, always consigning it to someplace in the future, the far-distant future.

And Vicente Serrano as her husband? Not likely! Her snooping had exposed a man adamant about choosing his own wife—if and when he wanted a wife.

Once again Alex couldn't help but wonder about the mysterious Silvia. Who she was and what she looked like. *Now you're really going too far,* she told herself.

Speculating about the girlfriend of a man you don't even care about. She glanced at her watch once more. Surely enough time had elapsed for a second try at an entrance. She left the bedroom and retraced her path downstairs. When she tapped on the open door of the parlor, the two men were huddled together on the sofa, arguing good-naturedly about sports. It was as though the earlier conversation had never happened.

"Buenas noches," Juan Carlos said warmly as both men rose to greet her. "Come, Alexandra, join me on the couch while Vicente brings us an aperitif. We've a fine sherry."

Although she had geared herself for the worst, the evening was pleasant, the three of them finishing their drinks, then moving to the dining room where they lingered over the meal. Juan Carlos probed into what Alex liked best about Ecuador and volunteered what he liked best about the States. Disney World and San Antonio headed his list.

She could understand how San Antonio, with its Latin influence, captured his fancy, but she couldn't picture the suave Juan Carlos in Bermuda shorts and a flowered shirt strolling through the crowds at Magic Kingdom. She smiled at the notion and at his unbridled enthusiasm. Somehow it made him seem much more human. By the time they had returned to the *sala* for an after-dinner coffee, Alex felt comfortable with him, comfortable enough to bring up the subject of Camila again.

"Señor Serrano, as you know, my goal in visiting your country is to gather material for my dissertation and for an article I'm writing."

"Ah, yes. Vicente told me about your discovery at the library. I've already contacted several of my colleagues in Quito. I feel certain we will locate a copy of *Andes Images* somewhere."

"I appreciate your going to so much trouble."

"It is my pleasure," Juan Carlos said.

Encouraged by his response, Alex decided to press her luck. "As much as I want the book, there's something else of equal importance. I want to talk with Camila Zavala. Do you or one of your colleagues know her?"

Alex caught the lightning-quick connection of Juan Carlos's eyes with his son's. The older man's voice was wary as he replied. "Alex. *Niña*. Whether I know her or not is irrelevant." He pulled a cheroot from a silver container on the side table. "As much as I would like to oblige the daughter of a revered business associate, in this particular endeavor I regret that I cannot."

Juan Carlos looked unhappy, and Alex felt a strange sense of guilt knowing she was responsible, even though she couldn't figure out why. Maybe Vicente and his friends were right, maybe she should forget about interviewing Camila Zavala. She could concentrate on the newly discovered novel, instead. It would be enough.

Anyway, it was obvious the Serranos had helped all they intended to, and just as obvious that Juan Carlos was distressed by her pushing for more. It would be better to talk of something else. "Very well." She smiled. "Vicente tells me you were born here at the hacienda."

"*Sí.* That was tradition until—"

"Pardon me..." The butler spoke from the doorway. "There is a telephone call for the young *señor.*"

While Vicente took his call, Juan Carlos entertained Alex with tales of his son's childhood, and the wariness began to fade from his expression. Both he and Alex were laughing when Vicente returned.

Juan Carlos rose from his chair. "Now, children, if you'll excuse me, I believe I'll retire." They stood, as well. "No, no, sit back down. It's early for the two of you. Talk and listen to music for a while." He walked over to a cabinet and pulled out a cassette, snapping it into a tape player. A love ballad by Roberto Carlos began. "Good night," he said as he left.

Once they were alone, an uncomfortable silence set in. Flames flickered in the stone fireplace, taking the chill off the night and—along with the music—giving the room a romantic atmosphere. But Vicente's mood seemed more pensive than romantic. He appeared to be in deep concentration. The tension was becoming unbearable to Alex, and she tried desperately to think of something to say.

She turned to face Vicente. "Problems?"

"No, not really." He eased back into the corner of the sofa, stretching out his legs in front of him. "I was just thinking . . . you seem to get along quite well with my father."

"He's a charming man."

Vicente shrugged. "What did you think of his comment that you'd make a beautiful bride?" He gave her no time to answer. "Perhaps you dismissed it as polite conversation—actually not so polite, since he embarrassed you. I assure you he meant no harm, but also that he meant exactly what he said." Vicente was watching her, apparently waiting for a reaction to his words.

Alex didn't know how to respond and determined it best to mask her confusing thoughts. She remained silent.

After a few moments, he said, "I'm afraid you've become embroiled in a minor domestic disagreement. In some ways I'm a disappointment to my father. He wants me to marry—soon. He fears he will die without ever holding a grandchild. His health is excellent, but he's thought more about death the past year, since my mother . . ." Vicente got to his feet and walked over to the fireplace to stoke the fire.

"Maybe he's right," Vicente went on. "As you once reminded me, there is a big difference in our ages. Granted thirty-four is not very old, but it won't be long before I'll be too set in my ways to share my life with anyone."

Alex regretted making the comment about their age difference. It would have been better to keep such observations to herself. She'd be careful to do so in the future. In the meantime, she couldn't help but wonder where Vicente was headed with this line of conversation. He'd already voiced his opinions on matrimony quite succinctly. Why was he bothering to bring up an apparently closed subject?

Vicente returned to the sofa and stared down at her. "Not only does my father want me to take a wife, he would also like to have a say in choosing her. An old tradition in Ecuador. Are your parents that interfering, as well? Or is there some protection in being one of six, instead of an only child?"

"A little maybe," she said guardedly, increasingly perplexed by this exchange. "But I think my parents will be pleased when I marry."

"I know it's simply because he loves me." Vicente forced a chuckle. "Occasionally I must remind myself that my *papi* wants only what is best for me. The problem is we don't always agree on what is best." He sat down next to her.

"I understand," she said, deciding that Vicente was warning her off, telling her not to jump to any foolish conclusions based on his father's words. Well, it wasn't necessary since she hadn't taken Juan Carlos seriously. It was time to change the subject. "Do you think your father will be more amenable to talking about Camila tomorrow?"

"Always Camila." His tone was stern. "I assure you he was being completely candid. You cannot count on his help to track your quarry."

"What about you?"

Vicente rested his elbows on his knees, pausing to study her as he answered the question. "I'm not sure what more I can do to assist you. Allow me some time to think about it. But no more of this tonight. Okay?" He smiled, and despite her apprehensions, Alex felt an uninvited rush of pleasure, then she mentally chastised herself for responding so.

She watched while he got up to change the music. Vicente Serrano was a complicated man, she concluded. Somewhat given to moods and accustomed to having his way. Again, Alex couldn't help wondering whether Vicente might not kiss her. After all, they were alone and—certain conflicts aside—there was definitely some chemistry between them.

But while he sat rather close to her on the couch, he didn't so much as hold her hand. It was as if his father's encouragement had had the opposite effect. His son was clearly not interested, and he didn't want Alex to get any ideas to the contrary.

A CLEAR, BEAUTIFUL morning welcomed Alex as she stepped out onto the veranda for breakfast. Juan Carlos was seated at a rattan-and-glass dining table, and he motioned for her to join him. Immediately a servant brought her a plate of freshly baked bread, plus coffee and half a mango.

While she ate, Juan Carlos pointed out the imposing snowcapped peak of Cotopaxi, an active volcano
not too far from the hacienda. Alex had her camera
with her, and she decided to take a few snaps of the
mountain using her zoom lens. As she attempted to
focus, she was surprised to spot Vicente crossing the
meadow with a man who looked like Pablo Rodríguez. No one had mentioned that Pablo was coming
from Quito.

"Is that Pablo with Vicente?"

"As a matter of fact, it is," Juan Carlos said. "I
wanted you to view the volcano up close. That's why
I asked Pablo to bring our plane down. He and Vicente have gone to check the flight plan, then Vicente
will fly you over the volcano on the way back to Quito.
It's the only way to really see it."

Once again Alex was amazed at the resources of the
Serranos. "A plane? I'm almost at a loss for words.
You've done so much already to make me feel welcome, and I hate to impose further. I'm taking up too
much of Vicente's time."

Juan Carlos brushed her comment aside with a casual flick of his tapered fingers. "Vicente can spare the
time if he wishes. In fact, the respite from work is
good for him." He freshened their coffee from a silver pot on the table. "Oh, by the way, Alexandra..."
Juan Carlos lifted the stack of newspapers on the table to reveal a book. He handed it to her. "I was able
to secure a copy of Camila's first novel. Pablo brought
it with him."

"This is wonderful!" Alex said. "I hardly know what to say. I'll return it as soon as possible. Or would you prefer that I reimburse you?"

"The book is yours to keep, and I would not consider taking your money. It pleases me to be able to give you something. But that's not all. I've been thinking about your search for Camila and about our conversation last evening."

"I'm sorry if I was presumptuous...."

"Please, do not be concerned. As I said, I've been thinking and I might have been too quick to refuse you."

"Then you'll help me?"

"In—how would you say?—a roundabout way. I cannot reveal Camila's identity. That right belongs to Camila alone. However, I will tell you this—the way to Camila is through my son. So go with Vicente today, see our country, then—" He stopped as footsteps approached the patio. She glanced up to see Vicente. "That is all I can say."

Vicente scowled. "I didn't mean to interrupt, but I forgot my sunglasses." He strode past them, appearing to be in a foul mood, Alex thought, his face set in a mask of irritation.

Was he annoyed about his father ordering the plane? Or because he'd heard part of their discussion? No matter. If he was upset, well, too bad. Served him right for all the aggravation he'd caused her. She had no interest in extricating Vicente from this situation. She'd suspected all along he could lead her to

Camila, and she planned on taking Juan Carlos's very good advice and looking to Vicente for answers.

Within seconds, Vicente reappeared on the patio, his sunglasses hooked in the buttonhole of his shirt. "If you can be ready, we'll depart in thirty minutes." He was standing near the low-hanging limb of a flowering shade tree, his arms crossed impatiently over his chest.

"I'll be ready," Alex said, folding her napkin beside her plate and rising. She went upstairs, brushed her teeth, touched up her makeup and repacked her small overnight case. When she came back out, Vicente was waiting, his own travel bag at his feet.

Juan Carlos walked over to his son and wrapped an arm around his shoulder. "You must take Alex to the coast, perhaps to Salinas. And don't forget the Galápagos. Her visit wouldn't be complete without a trip there."

Alex thought it would be wonderful to see the Galápagos—Ecuador's magnificent wildlife islands. It was there Charles Darwin had studied both plants and animals and used his findings as the basis for his theories in *The Origin of Species*.

She'd considered trying to visit the Galápagos while she was here, but the extra time and expense had deterred her. None of Camila's novels had been about the islands, so she didn't feel she could justify the trip. Would Vicente actually take her? From the expression on his face, he'd prefer another activity, such as dropping her into the mouth of that volcano!

"I promise you Alexandra's trip will be memorable, Papi," Vicente said, with a trace of irony in his voice. After Alex had bid Juan Carlos goodbye, Vicente escorted her to a golf cart where one of the hacienda's handymen waited to take them to the landing strip.

Vicente was quiet as they boarded the plane and he assumed the controls, Alex seated next to him. When she ventured a question about what Pablo would be doing in their absence, Vicente informed her he was driving the car back to Quito. He offered nothing more in the way of conversation and soon they were airborne, making several loops around Cotopaxi to give Alex ample angles and opportunities to photograph the peak.

"Where are we going now?" she asked when it was apparent they were leaving.

"To Quito. Contrary to the plans you and my father devised, I have no intention of playing tour guide again."

"Plans your father and I made? I knew nothing about this trip until I came downstairs this morning."

"No, of course not," he said sarcastically. "He dreamed all this up by himself." Vicente gave her a suspicious glance. "I have no idea how you manipulated my father so easily, but he certainly seems captivated by you."

"Manip— You're the one who's been doing the manipulating. Right from the moment you met me at the airport and spirited me off to your house!"

"It wasn't very difficult persuading you to stay."

"I didn't want to offend you. After all, you're a client of my father. For all I knew, custom called for—"

"Is that why you telephoned in the first place? So you could play up to my father?"

"Of course not! All I knew about the Serranos was that my father had business dealings with the two of you. And what do you mean 'play up to him'?"

"You know full well you've got him wrapped around your little finger."

"I know no such thing. And what if I did? What are you so worried about? That he'll help me find Camila?"

"Don't be silly."

"That's it, isn't it? Helping with the book was just a ploy. You refuse to allow him or anyone else to assist me! Why are you trying to keep me from her?"

"You're talking gibberish."

"I think I'm speaking quite clearly. Believe me, I regret making that telephone call. I've never been more frustrated in my life." Vicente might be the way to Camila, but Alex had had enough. She'd move to a hotel, start reading *Andes Images* and see about going home earlier than planned. She had plenty of material for the *Newsmakers* article. So she didn't have the interview. It had been a pipe dream, anyway. "How soon will we be in Quito?"

"About half an hour. Is that soon enough for you?"

"The question should be, 'Is that soon enough for *you?*'" she retorted, then turned her head to stare out the window. *I promise, Señor Serrano, soon you'll be free of my company forever.*

CHAPTER FIVE

"I WILL NOT permit it!" Vicente reached over and depressed the telephone's plunger, cutting off Alex's conversation with the hotel reservations clerk.

"Permit?" She slammed the receiver down, sorry she missed his fingers, and crossed to the window, determined to stay calm. She'd have none of his domineering ways—not anymore. He'd treated her like a cipher on the trip back to Quito, and now the first words out of his mouth were a command.

"You have no authority over me," Alex said. "You've been nothing but a hindrance in my efforts to find Camila, not to mention your boorish behavior this morning. You made it clear that I'm unwelcome, and I don't stay where I'm not wanted. There's no way you can keep me here, short of hog-tying me, but I don't believe even you'll go that far." She went back to the telephone and dialed again.

Vicente took the receiver from her, but this time his actions were less confrontational. "Forgive me. You're right. I have acted despicably. And I would never—" he paused "—hog-tie you."

The glint in his eyes and the slight smile belied his apology. Yet Alex knew that, for some reason, he didn't want her to leave. She was certain it was because of Juan Carlos. Vicente preferred to suffer her presence awhile longer to avoid any family conflict. His next words confirmed her supposition.

"My father would be upset if you left." He opened his mouth as though to say something else, but was obviously having a difficult time getting the rest of the message out. "And I, also," he finally said.

I'll bet, she told herself. Maybe for about five seconds. She wanted to throw his insincere words right back in his face, but realized it would just be spiteful. After all, she had accepted the Serrano hospitality in the first place, and if she stormed out now, Juan Carlos would be disturbed. Alex had to consider her own father, too. She just hoped she hadn't already somehow damaged his business relationship with the Serranos.

Realistically, she didn't have the option of moving, but she did have the option of leaving Ecuador. Thank goodness she hadn't asked *Newsmakers* to finance this expedition. At least she had some control over her agenda. Once Vicente headed for his office, she'd contact the airline about going home early.

Alex lifted her hands in a gesture of acquiescence. "Very well. I'll forget about the hotel." She turned and left, heading for her own room, her outward appearance one of calm resignation.

SIX MORE DAYS and I'll be gone. As she absentmindedly showered and applied her makeup, Alex dreaded each of those days. She'd spent the previous afternoon trying to secure an earlier flight, but practicality intervened when the airline clerk reminded her of the severe financial penalty for changing her reservations. Besides, every flight for the next few days was fully booked, and the best she could hope for was standby.

She lay back down on the unmade bed, thinking over her situation. Certainly she'd acquired enough information to write the article and also to improve her academic work, but she'd fallen short of her ultimate goal—a conversation with Camila. Despite Juan Carlos's cryptic comment about his son's being the key, Vicente hadn't helped her one iota, and he didn't seem likely to.

Yesterday, after the argument about her moving, Vicente had sequestered himself in the study. Later he'd gone to his office, not returning until early morning. Alex knew it was near dawn because she'd just finished reading *Andes Images* when she'd heard him come in. And he'd left again within hours.

While a part of her was grateful Vicente hadn't shadowed her like a prison guard, another part was inexplicably annoyed. Apparently he was confident she'd remain at his house in his absence. He'd probably even guessed she'd tried to get an earlier flight and been unsuccessful.

So how to endure the remaining time she had left in Ecuador? She could spend the rest of the morning on a first draft of the article. Then what? Going back to the university library would be unproductive. Should she contact a travel agency and inquire about tours of Quito? She really hadn't seen much of the capital city.

Vicente momentarily solved her problem, calling to tell her he'd planned a small get-together with a few friends that evening and asking her to attend. To help occupy her time during the day, Alex decided to follow through with the notion of dropping in on a travel agency. She'd also do a bit of shopping and buy some colorful balsa-wood parrots to take to her nieces and nephews.

A FEW FRIENDS! Alex tried to estimate the number of guests as she looked around the large salon. Certainly more than a hundred people had passed through those double doors leading from the hall, among them several dignitaries from the U.S. diplomatic corps, other members of the international community, business associates of the Serrano family and three familiar faces—Pablo and the Suttons.

Alex had given up hope that she'd meet with Camila, but now she was becoming excited at the idea that among all these people, there could be someone who knew the author—maybe even Camila herself.

If so, would she willingly reveal her identity to Alex? It was a possibility, one that Alex clung to. After all, how could a person who'd taken the effort to correspond with a young girl refuse to acknowledge her presence if the occasion ever arose? Alex envisioned being able to ask Camila why the letters had stopped, why the books had changed.

A smile formed on Alex's lips. This was what she'd been hoping for. But she did wonder if Juan Carlos had insisted that Vicente host the event to help her. Arranging a party like this would have taken her a month of planning, yet Vicente had managed it overnight. Or had it been something he'd scheduled weeks before but hadn't mentioned? Either scenario suited her. It was an opportunity Alex didn't plan on squandering.

She was standing in a corner chatting with Debbie Sutton and Wilson Roberts, one of the American Embassy staff. She had already tried to pick Wilson's brain on his knowledge of Camila, and now they were back to making polite small talk.

"So are you and Vicente old friends?" he asked.

"No, actually our fathers are longtime business associates."

"Oil?"

"Yes, my father is an equipment supplier," Alex said, trying to figure out how to wrangle an introduction to someone else she could interrogate when she noticed that Wilson's attention had been diverted. She followed his gaze and found it focused on a new arrival. A woman.

Not just any woman, either, but an incredibly attractive and dramatic one—dark, doe-eyed and dressed in glossy black taffeta with massive pearl-and-onyx earrings dangling halfway to her shoulders. She was a bona fide head turner, possibly the most beautiful female Alex had ever seen. So beautiful that Alex suddenly felt bland and underdressed in her pink silk sheath and matching pumps. For the first time in her life, she even experienced a wave of disappointment that the curls piled on top of her head were blond instead of black as midnight.

Alex watched as Vicente wove his way through the crowded room to greet this latest guest. Noticing his dimpled smile of welcome, the clasping of her hands in his, Alex fervently wished that this was not Silvia.

Somehow she knew her wish was wasted. The woman greeted Vicente with a proprietary kiss on the lips, then reached up to wipe away the smear of bright red lipstick she'd branded him with—the stroke of her thumb across his lower lip a caress in itself. She smiled radiantly as Vicente slipped her hand into the crook of his arm and led her in Alex's direction.

Alex was relieved she wasn't alone, that she would have Debbie and the embassy staffer as a buffer when she met Silvia. But her relief quickly dissipated as Wilson went to freshen his drink and Debbie suddenly spotted a friend across the room. Alex waited nervously, twisting her empty punch cup in the bottom of her palm and observing the couple as they made their way toward her.

"Alexandra Harper," Vicente announced when they finally reached her. "Alex, meet Silvia Valenzuela. I think you'll find you have much in common."

Silvia's smile of greeting showed a set of perfect white teeth. "So pleased to meet you," she said. "I hope you're enjoying your stay in our country."

Her words of welcome gave the illusion of warmth, but Alex detected coolness, distrust even, in those velvet eyes. "Very much, thank you," she answered, wondering what she could possibly have in common with this woman—other than the fact they were both female.

At that moment Pablo came up and planted a kiss of greeting on Alex's cheek. "Hello, Alex." Then he moved to kiss Silvia. "Hello, *bellísima*. Why don't you admit you're crazy about me and let me take you away from all this . . . this incessant luxury?"

Silvia rewarded him with a fetching laugh. "Just say the word, *señor*." She momentarily wrapped her arms around him, standing on tiptoe to whisper in his ear.

Pablo grinned as Silvia released him. "If only you were serious. Now, no more toying with my emotions. Tell me, what do you think of our visitor?"

"She is charming," Silvia said, her voice somehow transmitting a different message to Alex.

"Isn't she?" Vicente interjected, taking Alex's hand and bringing it to his lips.

His unexpected action shocked Alex, and her initial inclination was to demand an explanation, but for some strange reason she was also slightly pleased by the tender gesture. It was just the encouragement she needed in the face of this daunting woman.

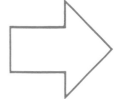

NO COST! NO OBLIGATION TO BUY!
NO PURCHASE NECESSARY!

PLAY "LUCKY 7" AND GET FIVE FREE GIFT

HOW TO PLAY:

1. With a coin, carefully scratch off the silver box at the right. Then check the claim chart to see what we have for you—FREE BOOKS and a gift—ALL YOURS! ALL FREE!

2. Send back this card and you'll receive brand-new Harlequin Romance® novels. These books have a cover price of $2.99 each, but they are yours to keep absolutely free.

3. There's no catch. You're under no obligation to buy anything. We charge nothing—ZERO—for your first shipment. And you don't have to make any minimum number of purchases—not even one!

4. The fact is thousands of readers enjoy receiving books by mail from the Harlequin Reader Service®. They like the convenience of home delivery...they like getting the best new novels months before they're available in stores...and they love our discount prices!

5. We hope that after receiving your free books you'll want to remain a subscriber. But the choice is yours—to continue or cancel, anytime at all! So why not take us up on our invitation, with no risk of any kind. You'll be glad you did!

NOT ACTUAL SIZE

You'll look like a million dollars when you wear this lovely necklace! Its cobra-link chain is a generous 18" long, and the multi-faceted Austrian crystal sparkles like a diamond!

PLAY "LUCKY 7"

**Just scratch off the silver box with a coin.
Then check below to see the gifts you get.**

YES! I have scratched off the silver box. Please send me all the gifts for which I qualify. I understand I am under no obligation to purchase any books, as explained on the back and on the opposite page.

116 CIH AQWK
(U-H-R-10/94)

NAME

ADDRESS   APT.

CITY   STATE   ZIP

7 7 7	**WORTH FOUR FREE BOOKS PLUS A FREE CRYSTAL PENDANT NECKLACE**
🍒 🍒 🍒	**WORTH THREE FREE BOOKS**
● ● ●	**WORTH TWO FREE BOOKS**
🔔 🔔 🍒	**WORTH ONE FREE BOOK**

DETACH AND MAIL CARD TODAY

THE HARLEQUIN READER SERVICE®: HERE'S HOW IT WORKS

Accepting free books places you under no obligation to buy anything. You may keep the books and gift and return the shipping statement marked "cancel". If you do not cancel, about a month later we'll send you 6 additional novels, and bill you just $2.44 each plus 25¢ delivery and applicable sales tax, if any.* That's the complete price, and—compared to cover prices of $2.99 each—quite a bargain! You may cancel at any time, but if you choose to continue, every month we'll send you 6 more books, which you may either purchase at the discount price...or return at our expense and cancel your subscription.

*Terms and prices subject to change without notice. Sales tax applicable in N.Y.

Vicente's kiss did not go unnoticed. The look Silvia gave him was frosty, a sharp contrast to her soft indulgent laugh. She snuggled against Vicente, in the process subtly disengaging his hand from Alex's. "You're causing your guest to blush, darling. She's not used to our Latin ways."

Alex had to admit she was somewhat disconcerted, but it was not her inexperience that made her feel that way. She was puzzled by this scene, unsure where all the players fit—herself included.

It brought to mind one of Camila's early pieces, a short story about a party such as this, with the protagonist standing off to the side, analyzing the guests. She wished she could similarly remove herself. From close range, all she could read on both Silvia's and Vicente's faces were unspoken challenges to one another.

Pablo seemed oblivious to any undercurrents. "I'm starving," he said. "If I can't have you, Silvia, I'm going to console myself with empanadas and champagne." He walked off toward the buffet table.

Silvia gazed up into Vicente's eyes. "Get me a drink, Vicentito," she cooed, "while Alex and I become better acquainted."

Her husky alto and leonine looks reminded Alex of Lauren Bacall—a younger, dark-haired, Spanish-speaking Bacall, that is. But the frosty undertones made Alex feel as though she needed to watch her back.

In Alex's opinion, Vicente didn't seem overly thrilled at the prospect of leaving the two of them alone. However, as host, he was obliged to cater to his guests, so he bowed slightly and left.

"Come, let's sit outside," Silvia suggested. "It's stuffy in here with this crowd of people."

Silvia was right. There were a lot of people in the room, and normally Alex would have jumped at the chance to escape the noise and crush of bodies. This time, though, she felt an inexplicable desire to remain where she was. Safety in numbers, perhaps. She had absolutely no desire to be alone with Silvia. *What's wrong with me?* she wondered. The woman had said nothing ungracious. Convinced she was overreacting, she meekly followed the Ecuadoran beauty out to the patio.

They sat in a couple of plush chaise longues set off to one side. Alex decided she'd better gather her wits before Silvia came to the conclusion that her companion was a complete dolt. "What do you do, Silvia?"

"Do?" The woman's eyebrows rose. She took a long cigarette from a silver case and lit it, the huge diamond dinner ring on her finger catching the light. "Hmm...nothing so mundane as a job, if that's what you're talking about." She brought the cigarette to her lips and inhaled deeply.

Even though Alex had always considered smoking a foul habit, she had to admit that Silvia made it seem an act of ultimate sophistication.

Silvia exhaled and went back to Alex's question. "I travel, I party, generally I live a contented life, thanks to three wealthy men—my father, my late first husband and my very recent ex-husband."

Well, she was frank, Alex thought. A little like Camila, whose unflinching candor contributed to her popularity.

"Hasn't Vicente told you anything about me?" Silvia flicked her cigarette ash into a large ceramic ashtray sitting on a nearby table.

"Actually he's said very little about you."

"Then, we're even, as you gringos would say. Likewise, he's told me very little about you."

There was a slight unpleasant inflection on the word "gringos." Silvia's aim was true—Alex *was* an outsider. Still, the other Ecuadorans she'd met seemed to accept her presence without question. None of them had acted as if she didn't belong.

Deciding she was being too sensitive, Alex gave Silvia a tentative peacemaking smile. She couldn't understand why Silvia made her feel so defensive. It was unusual for Alex to take such an immediate dislike to someone. Although reserved by nature, she'd always gotten along well with people.

"I can see," Silvia continued, "now that we've met, why Vicente attempted to keep you a secret." She tucked a strand of dark hair behind an ear and looked at Alex appraisingly.

"I'm afraid I don't know what you mean."

Silvia chuckled. "I've often teased him about his weakness for blondes. Nothing personal, mind you."

Nothing personal? Alex didn't need to be a Phi Beta Kappa to figure out that Silvia's comments were extremely personal. The woman viewed her as a competitor.

But Alex wasn't about to let the other woman's words hurt her, not when Silvia could possibly be of some use. The woman might not be likable, but she was Ecuadoran, from a prominent family and undoubtedly very social. If anyone knew Camila, she should. "So Vicente hasn't told you my purpose for visiting?" Alex asked pointedly.

"Something about the university, I believe," Silvia said in a dismissive tone, as if fearful Alex might be encouraged to elaborate.

"Only indirectly." Alex was pushing on, anyway, ignoring Silvia's obvious indifference. "I'm working on my doctorate in Latin American literature. Camila Zavala is the subject of my dissertation, and because of that, I've been asked to write a magazine article about her. I hope to meet and interview Camila while I'm here."

Unlike most of the others to whom she'd divulged her interest in Camila, Silvia offered no warning of the danger, no suggestion that it was a futile, reckless effort. Instead, she laughed. A low-pitched, somewhat musical laugh. "You *are* naive," she finally said. "Perhaps that's why Vicente finds you so refreshing."

Silvia's comment didn't catch Alex completely off guard, but it did interrupt her train of thought as she sat there counting to ten in an attempt to weather this latest round of sniping. Apparently Silvia didn't intend to let up on the artillery fire.

Fortunately Alex didn't have to make a reply, because Vicente had found them. He handed Silvia a glass of champagne, then said to Alex, "I notice you have no drink. Can I get you something?"

"A glass of mineral water, please."

He called out to a nearby waiter. Apparently he'd decided not to leave the two women unattended again.

Silvia patted the end of her chaise longue so that he would sit beside her. "Your guest is a delightful child, darling." She stroked Vicente's shoulder with her red-lacquered nails. "And so interested in Camila."

A frown crossed Vicente's face. A warning to Silvia?

Alex found the exchange fascinating. Silvia's motivation was plain enough—simple jealousy. Vicente's behavior was not so easily explained. Silvia was clearly a part of his life, yet he didn't treat her like a lover. And they acted as if they knew something about Camila that Alex didn't. She suspected that that something was Camila Zavala's identity.

So how was she supposed to react or respond to their exchange? She was a guest in the Serrano home with an obligation to behave with decorum. She'd have to pretend to be oblivious to what was going on and merely allow the situation to evolve.

She was glad to see that Silvia had put away the barbs and reverted to being charming in Vicente's presence. And Vicente seemed more amused than perturbed by Silvia's possessiveness. Like a lion with two lionesses, thought Alex with irritation. Why did she have the compulsion to be the one stroking the pride's lone male? Why did she feel jealous? For there was no other explanation for her barely controlled impulse to slap Silvia's hand away.

At that moment Pablo reappeared. "This is definitely unfair," he said. "Since when is the host allowed to hide away with the two most beautiful women at the party?"

"We were discussing Camila—" Silvia began.

"Well, my friend," Vicente interrupted, "now that you have evened the ratio, I'll take this opportunity to dance with Alex. If you'll excuse us..."

Here we go again, Alex thought. Vicente was back to playing his game of distraction, and just when Silvia seemed willing to lead the conversation in the desired direction. And he hadn't even bothered to ask Alex's permission as he pulled her away from Silvia and Pablo.

A small band was playing salsa music in an inner courtyard of the house. Vicente took her in his arms and twirled her around the tiled floor to the Latin beat. "So how does our way of socializing compare with what you're used to?"

"Much more elaborate. As a long-term college student my idea of a party is pizza and beer. But I've enjoyed the food and music, as well as meeting your friends.''

''I thought you would find them pleasant. And Silvia? What do you think of her?''

Alex paused. Why was he asking her this? ''She's very beautiful.''

''True enough. Nothing else to say?''

''I like her earrings.''

Vicente threw back his head and laughed. ''You women never cease to amaze me. Can't be together without a few sparks.''

''Hogwash,'' she retorted indignantly. ''That's a myth spread by men to keep females at each other's throats. I thought it was peculiar to my country, but apparently I was wrong.''

''So you're telling me you and Silvia 'hit it off,' as you *Norte Americanos* say? I wish it was true. Her life has been difficult the past few years. By the way, did she ask about your studies?''

''No. Did you expect her to?''

''Possibly. You see, she also majored in Latin American literature. That is one of the things you have in common.''

''Oh, really? So why did you pull me away when she mentioned Camila?''

''Did I?'' His expression was one of pure innocence.

''Don't bother with that guileless routine. It won't work.''

"But, Alex, Pablo appeared and I wanted to dance, that's all. I wasn't trying to impede your research."

"That's interesting, since you've done nothing but impede it since I arrived—though you did say you would think about helping me. Just tell me—is Camila Zavala at this party?"

Vicente smiled. "Surely you ought to be able to figure that out for yourself by now, *cariña*. You are as knowledgeable on the subject as anyone." The salsa music had ended and now a soft ballad was being played. Vicente pulled her closer and placed his cheek next to hers. The scent of lemony after-shave, along with a heightened awareness of his body against hers, filled Alex's senses, causing her momentarily to forget her goal. He might not be a large man, but she could feel the wiry strength of his shoulder beneath her hand and there was a decided firmness in the way he guided her around the floor.

Alex couldn't comprehend what this sudden closeness was all about. The possessiveness, the endearments. A strategy to make Silvia jealous was the obvious answer. But that explanation only brought more questions. Just then Pablo approached and tapped Vicente on the shoulder. "My turn," he announced.

Vicente released his hold and walked away, leaving them in the courtyard.

"I was bribed by the lady across the room," Pablo explained, nodding to Silvia who was standing just inside the door.

"It took a bribe to get you to dance with me? That's hardly flattering," Alex said, pouting prettily. But she did not chide him further because the look on his face told her he was hurt by Silvia's suggestion. Despite the teasing, Silvia was important to him.

Alex was grateful when the dance finally ended. Not because of any deficiencies on the part of Pablo—he was an agile and attentive dance partner—but because Alex needed time alone, time to think. The music was constantly shifting tempo and for the most part had been noisy and lively—too lively. She rejoined the guests in the large salon to take a break and catch her breath.

She filled a plate at the buffet table with empanadas, tiny meatballs and a delicious-looking seviche made from hearts of palm, then stood, back against a wall, sampling the food and watching the social interchange. *Was* Camila here?

"There you are." Debbie came up to join her. "I've been dying to find out how you fared with Silvia." She peered into Alex's face. "Well, no scratch marks. She must have let you off easy."

"I wouldn't say that," Alex confided with a laugh, Debbie's Texas twang making her feel more at ease. "You ought to see the puncture wounds on my back."

Debbie chuckled. "I figured she wouldn't be too keen on your being Vicente's houseguest. She considers him her private property."

"What's with Silvia, anyway? I'm no threat to her relationship with Vicente. Why the hostility?"

"Silvia doesn't really like any women. Maybe it's because she grew up without a mother in a household of men. Her father and three brothers spoiled her rotten. So did her first husband, I understand."

"Have you known her long?"

"Only as a passing acquaintance. She's never sought out female friends, but when I first met her, she wasn't quite so caustic around other women. Now, though, she seems to begrudge any woman her happiness. Probably because she's been so unlucky in love herself." Debbie stopped. "Enough of my amateur psychoanalyzing. Suffice to say men adore her."

"But why? Her tongue could qualify as a lethal weapon."

Debbie sighed. "I believe it's called the queen-bee syndrome. With women she's competitive, but around men she's different. Alan thinks she hung the moon. He can't understand why I don't agree. The truth is whenever I'm around her, I feel as if I just fell off a turnip truck."

"I can relate to that," Alex said. "And at least you helped me understand her attitude. I wondered what I was doing wrong."

"Well, rest easy. It wasn't anything you did. Actually it's a pity she has to be that way because a friendly Silvia would have a lot to offer. She's well-read, articulate, funny and supposedly she's game for anything. She travels all over South America—sometimes on a motorcycle, if you can believe it. I heard she even tried bullfighting once."

The women shook their heads in wonderment.

"Did you decide to take our advice and give up your Camila quest?" Debbie asked after a moment.

"I'm afraid not," Alex admitted. "I probably should have, since I'm getting nowhere. There have been more sightings of a dead Elvis than of a live Camila."

"I'm sorry," Debbie said.

Alan Sutton came up to take his wife away. "Excuse us, Alex, but we think I may have a business deal brewing in the next room."

Alex was left alone again to survey the guests. Someone in this room might be Camila Zavala. Vicente hadn't exactly said so, but he certainly hadn't denied it completely. The hairs on her neck prickled as that thought took hold and she allowed her imagination free rein, contemplating one woman and then another—the bosomy, grandmother type in the caftan, the Cher look-alike, the new bride whispering to her husband, the ambassador's wife. No, none of them fit her image of Camila.

Silvia reentered the room on the arm of a man. Alex remembered his name was Marco Poveda, and he appeared enchanted by his companion. But before long, Silvia seemed to tire of Marco, leaving him and wandering into the hall, and Alex's eyes followed her. Then, as she stood there watching Silvia, an idea struck her.

Silvia! The haughty beauty who spent all her time traveling and playing, the rich woman who mocked

herself, the daredevil riding motorcycles and challenging bulls. And, now that Alex reflected on it, Silvia's life paralleled that of a recent Camila heroine—
a woman who was the daughter of a rich man, the
widow of another. She'd even carried long filter-tipped
cigarettes in a silver case like Silvia. And those questions of Vicente's, asking her what she thought of Silvia. Was he insinuating that Silvia was Camila? Could
her idol really be . . . ?

Alex had a sinking sensation as the idea took hold.
She was afraid to breathe, as if breathing might make
it so. Was this to be the ultimate irony in an ill-fated
trip? She refused to accept the notion. Not by any
stretch of the imagination was Silvia a sensitive person, certainly not one capable of writing the enlightened passages in Camila's novels.

It was true Silvia had access to the necessary circles
of power. But what about the circles of poverty?
Could she move around the slums sporting that jewelry? Rough it with those fingernails? Alex couldn't
picture Silvia hacking through the rain forest with
those bloodred talons.

Besides, she was too young to have achieved so
much. Surely Silvia could be no more than thirty-five
or -six, and Alex had always pictured Camila as older.
Now she wondered why. It was possible that Camila
was in her thirties. In fact, it almost made sense. As
her father had reminded her, the difference in Camila's writing might simply be a reflection of the maturing of the writer.

But what about the letters? Those couldn't have come from Silvia. Alex felt certain about that. She might not know who Camila was, but Camila would recognize her. If Silvia had written the letters, then she wouldn't have treated Alex the way she had. Unless it was a ploy to keep from being unmasked, Alex reminded herself, trying frantically to make an unbiased assessment.

Everyone seemed to think that Alex had no chance of getting an interview with the novelist. And if Silvia was Camila Zavala, it was likely a dead issue. What had the woman called her? Naive?

Alex had never considered the possibility that she might meet Camila and not like her. No, her musings had all been sweet illusions. Camila would be a remarkably giving woman who, because of illness, travel, deadlines or whatever, had been unable to continue corresponding. Camila, when found, would be oozing with gratitude that Alex had cared enough to search for her. All that now seemed like a fairy tale, a childish assumption that was about as probable as Alex and Silvia becoming best pals.

Alex's initial reaction was to retreat to her room and fall into bed. Her second impulse was to pack her bags and forget all about this place, even if she had to camp out at the airport until a standby seat was available. She'd been foolish to come to Ecuador with the notion she'd actually talk to the elusive author. Sure she'd traveled on the pretext of being a reporter, but the *Newsmakers* article had just been an excuse. Her real purpose had been personal. Now the whole idea sounded simpleminded.

Camila Zavala may never have written to her at all. Someone working for her, a secretary or assistant, could have answered Alex's letters on Camila's behalf. There were many such possibilities, possibilities she hadn't even considered before.

Alex slipped through the crowd with the intention of going back outside. She needed some fresh air to clear her head.

She'd not quite reached the door when she heard the rustle of taffeta. Silvia and Vicente were practically at her side, yet neither had noticed her, so engrossed were they in whispered conversation. Alex was fascinated by its intensity, and she watched as they crossed to a far wall of the patio. She made her way to a spot nearby, concealed by shrubbery. Perhaps she'd been dim-witted in searching for Camila in the first place, but she'd make sure she kept her good senses now. Those two knew Camila Zavala, and Alex didn't plan to pass up what was probably her last opportunity to find the writer.

"I'll not stand for this," she heard Silvia hiss. "It's an abomination—parading the girl in front of my nose. What will everyone think?" Despite Alex's fluency, Silvia's rapid, angry Spanish was difficult to follow.

"Why should they think anything unless you've presented us as something we aren't." Through a break in the leaves of the bush Alex could see Vicente's hand resting on the concrete wall, his gold signet ring glimmering in the moonlight.

"I thought we had an understanding."

"I've not misled you. We've been friends—nothing more."

"Nothing?" Silvia's laugh was a quiet ripple, yet there was a bitterness to it.

"Think about it," Vicente said. "When we first met we were children, then suddenly you were married to my best friend. We became close because of him and we stayed that way even after Sebastián's death, even during your marriage to that crazy Argentine movie star. Only when you divorced him did we ever have what might be called a romance, and you'll have to agree it was short-lived." Vicente's voice was gentle, but firm. "It wasn't meant to be, Silvy. I never had any intention of being husband number three. Even if we were in love—and don't keep trying to deceive yourself that we are—you've always known of my feelings about the divorce."

"Your feelings. Ha! I believe you mean your father's feelings." A lighter clicked and the smell of smoke wafted through the air. Considering the woman's waspish tone, Alex wondered whether her gestures with the cigarette were as sexy as before.

"I am not my father's puppet," Vicente said impatiently. "He would never expect me to be. Certainly his position is clear and I respect it. It just happens that our opinions on most subjects are similar."

"And what about Alexandra Harper? Do the two of you agree on her, also? Which Serrano is responsible for her being here?"

"Alex is *my* guest."

"I'm sure," Silvia said in a condescending tone. "Or could it be that your *papi* sent for her?"

"He did no such thing and I suggest you cease speaking of him in that disrespectful manner. I will not tolerate it."

Alex had expected to hear Silvia continue to argue, but instead, her attitude changed and she sounded penitent. "I'm sorry, *mi amor*. I'm being foolish. Forget everything I've said. Forget all these people. Let's leave and go to my apartment—right now."

"Be serious. I cannot abandon my guests."

"Why not?"

"Ah, Silvia. You are forever willing to flaunt convention, to risk everything."

"I take risks only if the outcome is worth the gamble," Silvia said, her low, sexy voice returning. "I promise you the outcome would most certainly be worth it." Alex could hear the taffeta rustling again as if Silvia were nestling closer to Vicente.

"Don't waste your time on me." Vicente's hand left the wall, and he moved away from Silvia. "There are many others who find you irresistible, one in particular."

Pablo. Alex almost said the name aloud. She clamped her hand over her mouth as she realized how terribly embarrassing it would be to give herself away.

But she'd certainly discovered some interesting tidbits while snooping. Reporting, she corrected herself, trying to rationalize her behavior.

"And don't try to force me into a commitment." Vicente's voice was firm. "I refuse to be put between the sword and the wall."

"You've always liked the danger of that precarious position," Silvia countered. "You've always liked me because I do take risks, because I live on the edge. Don't try to deny it. A woman like Alexandra Harper would bore you."

"Maybe. Maybe not."

"Then your patience is improving."

"Perhaps it's that we have a different definition of boredom. The more I'm with Alex, the more I discover that in some ways, she and I are alike. Compatible."

"Surely you're not smitten?" Silvia's laugh sounded in the night air.

"It's less a matter of smitten and more one of respect. For instance, Alex has intelligence and, judging from what I've read of her dissertation, talent as a writer. Also she manages to be at once shy and talkative, diplomatic and assertive. . . ."

"Call it whatever you like, but sooner or later you'll tire of your young blond friend. Already she bores me and I've only just met her. I'll be relieved when she flies back north."

"Your claws are showing, little cat. But I suggest you sheath them. Alex will only be here a few more days."

"Too long. And," Silvia continued, "perhaps time enough to figure out Camila's identity." Her voice was now somber.

Alex could see the flare of Silvia's cigarette tip and moved away a couple of steps, trying to ensure she was not discovered. But she couldn't flee now.

"Do you plan to tell her?" Vicente challenged.

"Of course not."

"Then she won't find out," Vicente said. "I've managed to obstruct this damnable nonsense so far. I can manage a while longer." He leaned against the wall, his back to Alex. "You found her undertaking rather amusing earlier."

"Only because it seemed so implausible. Now I'm not so confident. You realize that if she discovers the truth, it could be trouble."

"I'll distract her with something or someone. Whatever it takes." Alex saw his hand move upward, the back of his fingers stroking Silvia's jawline. "Don't worry. Camila's identity will remain safe."

CHAPTER SIX

COULD IT BE? Was Silvia Camila? As much as Alex
wanted to deny it, the possibility gnawed at her. Alex
was back in her suite, tired of the party. Many of the
guests had already left, so her slipping out shouldn't
be considered rude.

Anyway, she doubted she'd be missed. When she'd
come upstairs the music had still been playing, there'd
been a sprinkling of couples on the dance floor, several people were clustered in a corner talking politics,
and a cadre of males had surrounded Silvia, who was
reclining on a sofa, holding court. Alex's departure
had probably gone totally unnoticed. After all, she
wasn't the hostess or the guest of honor, and right now
she wanted as little as possible to do with the host.

Vicente's actions continued to throw her off-bal-
ance. One minute she was contemplating him as a
lover, the next she was frustrated by his continued efforts to thwart her search for Camila.

And Alex hated to admit that jealousy played a part
in her dislike of Silvia, but even worse than the jealousy was her obsession with Camila. An obsession
that had led her to blatantly eavesdrop on a private

conversation, and allow her to consider something worse.

She rubbed the back of her neck, grateful that she hadn't given in to the impulse to search Vicente's office. She'd momentarily contemplated how easy it would be. Vicente and the servants were so involved with the party that no one would notice. She'd quickly go through his desk, his file cabinet, his telephone listings. Perhaps in one of those she'd find a clue.

Fortunately she hadn't succumbed to the temptation, but still couldn't rid herself of the guilt she felt for even thinking of doing something so reprehensible. Although she wanted to find Camila, it wasn't worth losing her self-respect. Her search would be strictly aboveboard from this moment on, she vowed.

She'd talk to Vicente again in the morning, after she'd had some time to decide what to say. Would it do any good just to come right out and ask him if Silvia was Camila? Would he tell her the truth? It was always impossible to anticipate Vicente's responses. One moment he was warm and attentive, the next, cool and dispassionate. At no time was she ever sure that he was telling her the whole truth.

Perhaps she should admit she'd overheard his conversation with Silvia. Maybe that would ease her conscience a little, and possibly convince him to be more forthcoming. But possibly it would only make him angry. That was a lot more probable. After all, eavesdropping wasn't very ethical.

Dressed in a flowing white batiste nightgown, her feet bare, Alex paced the bedroom floor. More than an hour had passed but she was still wakeful. She'd gone from flagellating herself to questioning what she would do if Silvia turned out to be her idol. Accepting the idea wasn't easy. It was as if her heroine had fallen from her pedestal with a loud crash. Alex walked over to the bedside table, picked up *Death of the Amazon* and casually leafed through the pages. The powerful words now seemed to mock her as she imagined them coming from Silvia.

Her vision of Camila had been so clear—a brave, Hispanic Joan of Arc, who like Saint Joan was leading an army, not to liberate Orléans, but to defend the rivers, jungles, mountains and people of her native continent. Now that romanticized vision was threatened.

Alex tapped a fingernail against the book's cover. How could a sophisticated socialite like Silvia have firsthand experience with the events described so vividly in these novels? If Silvia was the author, then she must have relied heavily on researchers, basing large passages of the novels on their accounts. The thought was even more disillusioning. Alex tossed the book on the bed in frustration and, yawning, slumped into a nearby chaise longue. She sat mulling over matters for half an hour before succumbing to her restlessness once more and resuming her pacing.

Finally she decided that there was no way Silvia was Camila. She'd sooner see Pablo or Vicente himself as the author. But that notion was equally preposterous. Camila's first novel had described the birth of a baby so vividly, so lovingly, the words could only have come from a woman. Would Silvia have felt that way when her first husband was alive?

Debbie said Silvia had changed. But could she have changed that much? Alex simply refused to believe it. After all, there were the letters to consider. They held an awareness, an empathy, that convinced her they had come from Camila's own hand. Those same qualities convinced her that Silvia could not be the woman she searched for.

Which meant that, if Vicente wasn't trying to protect Silvia's identity, he was either protecting someone else or deliberately undermining Alex's search just for the sport of it. Both prospects were troubling, but the idea he'd been toying with her hurt more. Why should he care if she sought Camila? She felt saddened at the possibility he could treat her so poorly.

She sat down at the dressing table and took the clips from her upswept hair. Languidly, she picked up a brush and began running it through the tangled waves. Just then a tap sounded at her door. She grabbed the matching robe to her nightgown and wrapped it around herself before answering.

"You slipped away too quickly, *cariña*," Vicente said. "We didn't have time to say good-night."

Cariña, my foot. Right now she was tempted to *cariña* him down the stairs with a well-placed kick to ease her frustrations. Alex was absolutely positive Vicente knew Camila's identity and would never share that knowledge with her.

"You were busy with your guests," was all she replied.

"Not that busy."

Vicente was leaning against the doorframe, his dark eyes dancing, causing Alex to wonder what he was up to now. She wished she was clairvoyant, because it was obvious he was poised to play out his latest effort at distraction. Considering just what that might be made Alex nervous. "Well, I'll bid you good-night, then," she said, hoping he'd take the hint and go away.

He smiled. "It's still early. Come have a nightcap with me. We can even talk about Camila."

How clever, she thought. Enticing her with her favorite subject. Well, he'd brought up the topic, she might as well seize the opportunity. "That could be interesting. Perhaps you'll expound on your insinuations that Silvia and Camila are one and the same."

"Silvia?" His voice was calm. "That's an intriguing notion. But on second thought, maybe we should save discussions of Camila—and Silvia—for another time. Come share a glass of brandy with me. I need to relax now that everyone's gone."

Alex's first inclination was to refuse, but since he'd acted just as she'd expected, she figured watching his diversionary maneuverings would be entertaining. "Okay. Allow me a couple of minutes to dress."

"You're fine as you are."

"I'd be more comfortable in something else. Give me five minutes. I'll meet you in...?"

"The library," he supplied.

When she entered the small room, Alex had to suppress a smile at the dimmed lights, which only faintly illuminated the book-lined walls, and the soft romantic music playing in the background. She might not be as educated in the ways of love as she was in literature, but this was a seduction scene if she ever saw one. Vicente's attentions confused her. At the party he'd apparently been using her to ward off Silvia. What was his reason now?

Vicente, sitting on the sofa, rose to meet her and gestured for her to join him there. Alex eased onto the soft leather, resting her back against the cushion and tucking her legs under her.

Play with fire and you'll get burned. She'd heard her father repeat that adage numerous times. The reminder seemed appropriate, because the atmosphere in the room was definitely combustible. She would need a clear head to avoid igniting a blaze. As disturbed as she might be over Vicente's machinations, it was becoming more and more difficult for her to ignore the physical attraction between them.

He poured Cognac into lead-crystal snifters and passed one to Alex, then sat on the cushion beside her. "You look very beautiful." His eyes took in her leggings and cotton-knit shirt. "But I preferred what you were wearing a few minutes ago. You seemed positively ethereal in it."

"Thank you," she said, trying to keep an indifferent tone. She took a swallow of brandy for courage, then twirled the glass in her hands studying the small eddy created by the motion.

They were both silent for several moments before Vicente said, "You've less than a week left in Ecuador."

She nodded.

"What do you plan to do with your time?"

"Except for the coast, I've gone to most of the places I planned to," Alex told him. "I really haven't seen much of Quito, however. After that incident..." She shuddered, not wanting to talk about what had happened when she was looking for Camila's first novel. "There are landmarks and churches I still want to visit."

"I'll take you."

"Please, no, I didn't mean..." As confused as she felt right now, it would be better if he wasn't at her elbow all day. There was that darned undercurrent she had to keep fighting. Why did it seem to be getting worse all of a sudden?

"Do you object to everything, Alex? There's no reason I shouldn't escort you."

"I was thinking about your work. I've taken you away from it too often."

"The work will wait."

She knew that wasn't true. Vicente frequently closeted himself in his study after she'd gone to bed, not leaving until well after midnight. She wondered if his business was this demanding all the time or if, despite the disclaimer, her presence had created problems. Apparently, though, he was escorting her come hell, high water or a full calendar.

As a practical matter it would be much more beneficial to see Quito with a native, instead of from a crammed charter bus listening to the practiced patter of a guide. This would likely be her one and only visit, she thought with regret, suddenly realizing that she'd grown to love the city with its tropical beauty and balmy weather.

It would be a long time before she could afford to take another trip. Twelve months from now she planned to be teaching at a small university. As a lowly underpaid instructor, she wouldn't be traveling out of the state, much less out of the country.

Her parents had invested a great deal of money in Alex's education and that of her five sisters. Although the outlay did not pose hardship for them, it did mean giving up some of the luxuries others took for granted. Alex was determined to be financially independent of her family once she graduated. She'd live entirely on her own earnings.

So now, while she was here, she would take advantage of the opportunity—do a little more research, some tourist activities and maybe even exact some revenge on Vicente by running him ragged. Those were her reasons for acquiescing, she told herself. As well, there was still a possibility—slight though it might be—that she would locate Camila through Vicente. "Okay," she said.

"You amuse me, Alex. Every decision is pondered. I like a woman who thinks before she speaks." He finished his brandy, then stood. "By the way—" He picked up a notebook from the table beside him "—I'll return this now. It's a remarkable effort." It was her dissertation.

"You're very generous," she said. She hadn't anticipated a compliment when Vicente had asked to see the draft. If anything, she'd expected veiled criticism. Still, he *had* told Silvia that she was talented.

"Merely truthful. Now, we'd better get to bed. I need to rise early to make a couple of phone calls and rearrange some appointments."

"THIS IS MY FAVORITE church." Vicente pointed across a broad plaza at La Iglesia de San Francisco. The plaza was a now-familiar montage of street vendors hawking everything from fruits and vegetables to clothes, cookware and jewelry. The selling never stopped, even on Sunday.

"It's my favorite," he went on, "mainly because of its legend. The story goes that a local named Cantuña was awarded a contract to erect the structure by a certain date. The night before the deadline, the job wasn't finished and Cantuña was frantic. El Diablo—the Devil—came to him, agreeing to complete the church in exchange for Cantuña's soul—"

"Oh, I remember that story," she interrupted. "Desperate, Cantuña accepted the bargain and El Diablo sent thousands of little red devils, *diablitos*, to do the work before morning."

"Right," he said. They walked along, Vicente obviously enjoying the sharing of the story. "By daybreak the church was finished and Cantuña's soul belonged to the Devil. But as he was inspecting it, he discovered that a single stone in the bell tower was missing, which meant the Devil hadn't honored his part of the bargain and Cantuña got to keep his soul."

"I think every country has its own version of that tale."

Vicente smiled and winked. "But ours is the true one. Would you like to see the site of the missing stone?"

After a brief tour through the church and an examination of the bell tower, they strolled back to the car, passing through the Plaza de la Independencia. Alex paused to take a picture of the President's Palace. She was amazed that she could walk right up to the front door without restriction. "Back home an ordinary citizen would never get this close to the White House except as a member of an approved tour group," she said, studying the guards in their plumed hats standing at the doorway.

Next they wound around the Panecillo, a hill in the middle of the city. Camila had written Alex that she could see her house from the base of the giant statue of the Virgin of Quito, which stood on the hill, and

Alex wanted to experience the sight with her own eyes. As they drove closer to the imposing landmark, Alex felt a sense of awe, then dismay as she turned to view the city laid out below. Sure Camila had seen her house—and everybody else's house, too. You could view the whole cursed city from up there!

It was dark when they returned to Casa Serrano. To Alex it seemed they'd visited every church, every museum, every art gallery in Quito. She had been hoping that Vicente would be "toured" out. Instead, Vicente, still chipper, was suggesting a visit to one more place, forcing her to beg for mercy.

He'd been infuriatingly charming and solicitous, smirking inwardly no doubt, as she slid into total exhaustion. So exhausted, in fact, that it was too taxing to maintain a posture of indifference.

"Tired?" He twisted in her direction, propping an arm on the steering wheel.

"A little," she admitted. "And my feet are killing me."

"Poor Alex. Go put on something comfortable and I'll have Luisa serve dinner."

As Alex showered and changed clothes, her suspicions began to reemerge. Vicente had been altogether too congenial. He had once again succeeded in distracting her from her quest. Was Silvia indeed the person she sought? Alex was going to press him for some answers while they ate.

Taking to heart Vicente's suggestions about dressing comfortably, Alex put on a pair of sweats and some loose-fitting slides for her aching feet, then went to join him. It was a simple meal—soup, cheese and fruit—and they were having coffee when she decided to bring up Silvia.

"And what is it you wish to know about her?"

Alex hesitated. She couldn't decide how to begin. Several unsuitable questions were running through her mind. The most persistent one was more suited to a tabloid than to *Newsmakers*. What does Silvia really mean to you?

"At a loss for words? Perhaps I can provide some answers without your asking." He smiled. "Silvia has been part of my group of friends since childhood. I worry about her. She is not a happy woman—and that is partially my fault."

"Would you care to explain?"

"It's a sad fact. Many people accuse her of being selfish, irresponsible, incapable of love, but that was not always so. She loved her husband Sebastián, and she was a devoted wife to him. Tragically he was killed when a plane owned by us went down in the jungle. Sebastián was making a trip I should have taken, doing a favor for me when he lost his life. Silvia was never the same."

"So you feel responsible for his widow."

"Yes, but that responsibility does not extend to becoming a substitute husband. It would be folly for many reasons. Even though I care for her."

"Do you love her?" Alex blurted out, startling even herself with the question.

"Does it matter?"

"To me? Of course not. I shouldn't have been so personal." Shocked, Alex realized that it *did* matter. But how could she explain this to him when she herself didn't understand? Besides, he hadn't denied loving Silvia. He'd simply evaded the question by posing one of his own. There was no point in Alex's pursuing the topic and risking an answer she didn't want, so she changed the subject. "I'm grateful to you for showing me Quito."

"You're welcome. And soon we must go to the equator so you can be photographed at the Mitad del Mundo monument, one foot in each hemisphere. For now, how about a swim? We've waited long enough for our food to settle."

"Oh, no, I'll freeze. I'm not used to swimming when it's so cool."

"I'll see that you don't get cold."

Alex glanced at him, wondering if he was basing his guarantee on the pool heater or himself. "Another time, perhaps." Alex rose from her chair. She might not be in total control of her faculties, but one thing was certain—being half dressed in the moonlight with Vicente was not a good idea. "I think I'll just say good-night."

ALEX SLEPT LATE, the digital clock indicating half past nine when she first opened her eyes. The tightly drawn curtains had cloaked the room in a comfortable darkness. As she lay in bed trying to convince herself to get up, she realized that for the umpteenth time Vicente had put her off. The man was a master. Alex had been so unsettled about his remarks about Silvia that she'd given no thought to Camila.

But now, refreshed from her sleep, Alex was clear-headed and thoughtful. Once again the notion that Silvia was Camila came to her. She hadn't asked how long it had been since Silvia's first husband died. It was possible that event could have stopped the letters, could have changed the style of her writing. Had grief transformed her, made her hard and uncaring?

Alex had never experienced the loss of someone she loved. Her four grandparents and all her aunts and uncles were still living. How could she understand such suffering when she had no frame of reference?

With renewed determination, she decided to interrogate Vicente as soon as she saw him. No diversions, digressions or distractions this time. If Silvia was Camila, Alex planned to know it before another sunset.

She ran into him unexpectedly in the dining room. By this hour, he should have been at the office, giving her all day to rehearse the confrontation. Instead, it appeared he'd slept in, also. He offered her a chair, then poured her a cup of hot milk with coffee. As soon as she was seated, Alex blurted out her question about Silvia.

Vicente's response was a look of amused incredulity. "I thought you were convinced she was not Camila. I'm intrigued you're reconsidering, but I assure you Silvia is not. She would be the first to admit that she and Camila are complete opposites. And Camila would be the second. Silvia is the ultimate aristocrat, nothing more. She has no desire to be anything else, nor have anything to do with anything else."

"What better disguise for a person who wants her identity to remain hidden than to pose as someone far removed from the hoi polloi?"

"I vow to you, Alex, Silvia is not Camila."

"Then why were you leading me in that direction at your party?"

"I'll admit I was trying to confuse you. Let's just say that your mysterious author does not want to be found. I wish you would leave it at that."

"I can't. I've admired Camila's writing for too long and can't just walk away without speaking to her. All I want is an interview. And frankly I'm not sure you're being truthful with me."

He seemed to take no offense at her accusation, merely shaking his head in response. "Well, if you're determined to believe that Silvia is Camila, then I will arrange a meeting so you can present your suspicions to her. Is that what you wish?"

Alex didn't answer immediately as she silently considered the alternatives. Vicente would think her ridiculous if she backed off after her ardent speech, but she wasn't certain she did want to talk to Silvia. In fact, she wasn't sure of anything anymore.

He touched her shoulder. "What do you want, Alex?"

"I don't know," she said. "Sometimes the illusion is best left alone. In this situation that's probably the case. Perhaps, despite what I said, I wasn't meant to know the real Camila. She's made such a difference with her writing—exposing political corruption and ecological destruction, increasing awareness. Most likely she's been successful because of her anonymity.

"Although I have no intention of revealing her real name, I might accidentally offer a clue to her identity and provide others with a means of locating her. I don't want to destroy Camila. I want to protect her." For others, she thought. Silvia might or might not be Camila. Regardless, Alex's fantasy was ruined. She realized now that the writer—whoever she was—was not a paragon, but a regular person with all the faults and foibles of any human being.

"You really are an idealist, aren't you?" He was watching her intently, his expression soft.

"A rather battered one at this point," she admitted wryly.

"Well, let me reassure the battered idealist. Silvia Valenzuela is not Camila Zavala."

For some reason, this time she believed him. Whether because she wanted so desperately for Camila to be someone else or merely because he looked so sincere, Alex didn't know, but she accepted his words as fact. "And I don't suppose you're going to put me on the right track?"

He shook his head. "I can't, *querida*. So what happens now?"

"My plane reservation is for Friday. I'm obviously not going to find anything else, so it's time to get to work. I'll probably spend the remaining hours writing."

He took her by the wrists. "I've a better idea. You mentioned the coast as being one of the places you wished to visit. Let's finish off your stay in style. I can get away for a couple of days. We'll fly to Guayaquil in the morning, drive to Salinas and spend the night, then get back with room to spare for packing."

"That...that wouldn't be smart," she answered hesitantly, unsettled by his closeness and the unexpected invitation. She tried to pull away, but Vicente didn't release her. His grip was firm, yet gentle, and her response to his touch brought to the surface that irrepressible attraction. Alex gave him a quick smile and tried to shift the conversation to something that would help her feel less vulnerable. "Thank you, anyway. You've been very gracious to put up with me."

"It's been my pleasure." He was now stroking the insides of her wrists, an intimate gesture that was affecting Alex more than she dared to admit. "Tell me, what do you think of Vicente Serrano?" he asked.

Alex tilted her head. "Somehow I suspect there are layers no one knows."

"Layers peel away when two people become friends. Are we friends, Alexandra? I'd like to think so."

"Perhaps we're starting to become...friends, although we still have much to learn about each other. It's apparent we're from two different worlds."

"Are we?" His thumbs continued to caress her wrists.

"Of course. Our cultures are quite dissimilar." It was important she remember this, but the time she'd spent with Vicente was making it more difficult for her to keep such things in mind. Was she becoming too caught up in the moment? "I'm a liberated woman, and—"

"And I'm a macho Latino?"

"I didn't say that."

"No, but I suspect you were thinking it. Don't let appearances deceive you, Alex. Get to know me better. Let me take you to the seashore."

Alex was tempted. This time he wasn't using Camila as a lure. Instead, he'd as much as admitted he'd like her to go for himself. She'd once taunted him about the differences in their ages, but now twenty-five and thirty-four didn't seem so far apart. Yet, along with the appeal of being with him, there was also an element of fear.

Vicente Serrano was a woman's man—the kind of man who always had a female pining after him. If not Silvia Valenzuela, then someone else. If Alex accompanied him, it might soon be her. And then what? The potential for a broken heart was great.

Nevertheless, she found herself weakening. As she wrestled with her voice of reason, Alex had to admit that she wanted to go. "Are you sure you can get away?"

"No problem. We can make a fast trip to the equator this morning, then I'll go to the office this afternoon and take care of any business details. We can leave for Salinas early tomorrow."

CHAPTER SEVEN

THEY FLEW in the small private jet to the port city of Guayaquil, then drove a short distance along the coast to the resort of Salinas, where they would spend the night. To Alex's surprise, they were staying at a third Serrano residence, not as imposing as the others, but spacious and elegant nevertheless.

Dinner was served on a flower-bedecked terrace with pungent citronella candles providing soft illumination. Relaxing in their cushioned patio chairs, Alex and Vicente sipped sparkling wine and watched the foamy Pacific waves gently wash the beach. When a breeze ruffled Alex's hair, Vicente reached over from his chair to brush a wayward strand off her face.

"You're very beautiful tonight," he said. "The candlelight has turned your hair to gold and added a special shine to your eyes."

Alex groped for a glib retort to deflect his comments and lessen the sexual tension, but she wasn't a glib person. In fact his nearness so disturbed her, she was almost tongue-tied.

Rising from her chair, she moved to the wall of the terrace. Below, an old man and a boy walked along the sand, the man carrying fishing poles and the youngster proudly hoisting the catch of the day. The bright garish moon hovered over the eastern horizon.

Vicente left his chair and followed her to the railing. "Have I disturbed you with my compliments?"

Alex gave a quivery little laugh, one that didn't even sound as if it belonged to her as she fumbled for a response. She didn't know what to say. Logic told her to be coy. But she didn't feel one bit logical; instead, feelings she'd been trying to suppress seemed to be assaulting her from all directions. Every neuron, firing madly, was propelling her into his arms. Her only armor had been maintaining an emotional distance, but now Vicente had traversed that distance, and Alex's protection had vanished.

He lifted her chin and kissed her lips gently. "Is that what you're afraid of?" he whispered. "Or is it this?" Grasping her shoulders in his hands, he pulled her to him and his lips sought hers in a demanding kiss.

An unfamiliar languor passed through her body as all trace of reason faded. And as she put her arms around him to tighten the embrace, any of the objections she might once have voiced, vanished. And she no longer cared.

If she'd been asked previously, Alex would have declared her life to be fairly complete. But now, as each new caress brought a heightened intensity of response, she realized what she'd been missing and what she wanted more than anything was Vicente's lovemaking. Abruptly he released her and stepped back.

"What's wrong?" she asked, her voice almost a groan.

"You...you're what's wrong. You make it difficult to remember my intentions are honorable. I didn't bring you here to seduce you." He trailed a finger down her cheek. "Although it's a very appealing idea." Walking back to his chair, he took a final swallow of wine from the glass on the table. "Perhaps it's time to say good-night, before something happens we both might regret."

Alex lay in bed later replaying those moments with Vicente. If he hadn't put a stop to the caresses, she'd have spent the night in his bed. She'd wanted to spend the night in his bed. So why had he called a halt?

His excuse may have been noble, but Alex doubted it was the real reason. Despite her growing attraction, every move, every word from Vicente was immediately suspect. The romancing could simply be part of his strategy to keep her mind off Camila. And by allowing herself to fall in love with him, Alex would be setting herself up for heartache.

Today had been idyllic, if unrealistic. Oklahoma might be only an airplane ride away from Ecuador, but there was more than mere miles separating the two. And even if those geographical barriers could be overcome, there was a bigger problem—the distrust that still hung between them. Unfortunately the attraction she felt for Vicente was making it increasingly hard to keep that concern in mind.

As maddeningly uncooperative as he'd been about Camila, she felt a camaraderie with Vicente, a compatibility. Sightseeing in Quito, the peaceful walk along the beach earlier that day, the afternoon spent reading. Many men would have considered such pursuits boring, but Vicente hadn't acted bored. He'd seemed to welcome the respite from work. Was it simply wishful thinking or were they more alike than she'd originally thought? Or worse, had she taken some overheard words between Vicente and Silvia and twisted them to her own purpose?

No, it wasn't just her imagination. They were both committed to their careers and families. They were also of the same religion. Sufficient reasons to pursue a relationship, but not sufficient enough to put aside real concerns.

Why hadn't he made love to her? Was it because he simply didn't want to? As she turned the thought over in her mind, Alex knew that wasn't the case. She might be inexperienced, but even a novice could see that Vicente had been as affected by their kisses as she. Why then had he stopped? Perhaps she'd have to accept his explanation after all. She was the daughter of Scott Harper; Vicente might consider making love to her a breach in form that could jeopardize his business relationship, as well as a violation of the caretaker role he'd assumed.

So what did the future hold? The answer was sadly clear—there was no future. For sanity's sake, all this togetherness had to cease. She couldn't take much more. Alex might not always trust his motives, but during their last few days together, she'd fallen in love. And she feared the love she felt for Vicente might never be experienced with another man.

The only practical solution was to get out while her dignity was still intact. She might have lost her heart and her head, but at least she hadn't lost her pride. Not yet, anyway. So it was time to go. The day after tomorrow she would return home, to her friends and family. And once she'd handed in the *Newsmakers* article, she'd get back to her studies. Oklahoma was where she belonged. Easy to say, but more difficult convincing herself that she would ever be content with the existence she'd known there. She and Vicente might live in two different worlds, but living without him now seemed impossible.

Alex switched on the lamp and picked up her glasses and a book. She needed to keep her mind occupied. But the words didn't hold her attention. Soon her mind was back on Vicente. *One more embrace. I need him to hold me once again before I go.*

Whether it was her own restlessness or the beckoning of the outgoing tide, Alex didn't know, but she was compelled to go out to the terrace. She slid open the glass doors of her bedroom and stepped outside, her soft cotton nightgown whipping against her legs in the ocean breeze.

Vicente was there, a few yards away, leaning on the railing and staring off into the night, oblivious of her.

When she approached him, he turned, their eyes meeting as he took her into his arms.

Alex felt as if life had been preparing her for this moment—to love and be loved by Vicente Serrano. He was whispering endearments in Spanish, and she responded with her own. Now his lips were on hers, his body pressed against hers, only his silk bathrobe and her thin nightgown separating them. She eased her hand under the collar of his robe, feeling the dampness forming on his skin, the vein throbbing furiously in his neck.

A demand for oxygen eventually caused them to break the kiss. Vicente nestled his chin in Alex's hair. "Alex, darling," he said, his voice tender, "this cannot be. You have never been with a man."

"How do you know?"

"I know, *querida*."

"Well, I don't care," she protested, her voice almost a whimper.

He leaned away to look into her eyes, his breath still uneven. "Someday you will."

"But what if I'm in love with you?"

"I'd say we'd have to blame such thoughts on the stars. They're making us wish for what we cannot have." He gently kissed her temple. "Don't try to tempt me any more than I already am. As much as I crave you, your innocence is a gift I refuse to accept. Now go back to bed and let me stay here and recover my good sense."

Alex pleaded silently with her eyes, but Vicente deliberately averted his gaze. Realizing that further argument would be futile, she obeyed his request and returned to her room.

She'd expected to dissolve into tears of frustration and rejection—her eyes had been welling when she left him. But the tears never came, and surprisingly she drifted into slumber almost immediately.

CORAL STREAKS of dawn covered the sky when she awoke. She lay there, plagued by indecision. Should she dress, go to the kitchen and act as though nothing had happened? Or should she wait for Vicente to seek her out, then follow his lead? She'd been the one who initiated their middle-of-the-night lovemaking, but Vicente had once again put a stop to it. Alex wasn't accustomed to morning-after misgivings.

Her worries proved unwarranted, because soon after, Vicente knocked and announced through the closed door that he'd received a call from his office and he needed to return to Quito as quickly as possible. He didn't offer further explanation, nor did he join Alex for breakfast. Instead, he begged off to make more calls. She doubted he'd been summoned by business. It was clear that Vicente just wanted to escape from her.

Suddenly it seemed as though the hours she had left in Ecuador started melting away before her eyes. Yet Vicente demonstrated no concern that their days together were coming to a close. He was subdued during the trip back to Quito, answering her every attempt at conversation with monosyllables. Dropping her off at Casa Serrano, he tarried only a moment to touch her cheek and say, "Alex, I'm sorry, but it would never work, don't you see?"

His eyes were troubled as he spoke, the situation clearly awkward for him. This was a side of Vicente Alex hadn't seen before. Obviously he didn't want a relationship with her and was trying to tell her as diplomatically as possible. Dejectedly she watched as he drove away.

Alex made one final visit to the library to check a reference she'd missed, then spent the rest of the afternoon packing. When she heard Vicente's car door slam, she went back downstairs. She might as well give him her thank-you speech now. Her flight home was fairly early the next day, and she might be rushed for time in the morning.

Ever gracious, Vicente asked her to join him in the library. He poured drinks—white wine for her and a vodka and tonic for him—apparently attempting to have her stay end on a cordial note. Then, before any real discussion could take place, the phone rang and he excused himself. "I'm expecting a call from my father." Taking his drink, he went into his study and didn't reappear.

Alex nibbled at the meal Luisa provided, hoping that Vicente would join her. When it became clear he wasn't going to, she went back to her suite. Well, that was it, she thought. Goodbye, and don't let the door

hit you on the way out. As she was closing the draperies, she gazed through the window at the now familiar panorama of lights extending up the
mountainside where they seemed to meld with the
stars. Somewhere out there was Camila.... Alex stood
for a few moments musing about the writer, then her
thoughts returned to Vicente.

It occurred to her that he'd realized her feelings
about him had changed and so he was avoiding her.
After all, she had been rather uninhibited—almost
throwing herself at him on the balcony. He was probably concerned that she'd start pushing for a more serious relationship. Putting him between the sword and
the wall, just as Silvia had.

The more she dwelled on it, the more Alex wondered if his bachelor status was no accident. He'd obviously had great success avoiding entanglements,
despite a father trying to engineer them. She was embarrassed to think he had categorized her as desperate to entrap him. If so, he should be pleased that
tomorrow she'd be gone and no longer posed a threat
to his way of life.

Early the next morning Alex was in the kitchen, using the telephone to summon a taxi. As she dialed, she
heard a rumble of thunder.

Securing a taxi by telephone was not an easy task in
Quito, the accepted method being simply to flag one
down from a busy street corner. But there were no
handy corners in Vicente's suburban neighborhood.
Nor was walking to one in the rain with several pieces

of luggage an option. Eventually Alex prevailed upon the bell captain at the Hotel Colón, who agreed to dispatch a cab to the residence.

As she hung up the phone, Alex realized that when giving directions for the driver, she'd automatically spoken in Spanish. In two short weeks she'd not only adapted to the change in language, but had easily acclimated herself to many of the cultural differences between her country and Ecuador.

It was not difficult to imagine living here and fitting in—but there was no point in even considering that. Her South American adventure was over. Soon she'd be back in wintry Oklahoma City resuming her old life—and someday she'd convince herself that she'd gotten out of this experience relatively unscathed.

Her luggage was packed and waiting in her room and with luck, she'd be able to slip out before the household awoke. Perhaps it was a coward's exit, but Alex couldn't endure a parting scene with Vicente. Her face might give away the unhappiness lying just below the surface and confirm to him just how much she did care. She'd written him a polite note and left it on the dresser in her room. That would have to suffice.

"Señorita, buenos días," a sleepy-eyed Luisa greeted Alex as she carried her laptop computer and hanging bag into the foyer. "I'll make breakfast."

"Gracias, but don't bother," Alex answered. "I'll wait and eat something on the airplane. A cab is on the way. Will you let me know when it arrives?"

Luisa looked dubious, but nodded agreement.

Alex headed back to her bedroom. She preferred to linger there before taking the rest of her luggage out. Luisa had been warm and friendly during her stay, but Alex wasn't up to conversation. As she passed through the house, she glanced out a window, taking one last look at the garden, barely visible in the gray dawn. It was raining in earnest now and a thick mist blanketed the mountains. The dreary weather matched her mood. She only hoped it didn't delay her flight.

"Stealing away like a thief in the night, instead of saying goodbye?" Vicente's appearance startled her. His eyes were somewhat bloodshot and his clothes were rumpled, as if he'd been up all night.

Even though she'd rationalized her behavior, Alex knew his words rang true. She did feel rather like a criminal. "I didn't want to disturb you."

"You've done nothing but disturb me since you arrived, *querida.*" His eyes were red rimmed, but they shone with intensity.

A discreet cough sounded behind them. "*Perdón, señorita.* Your taxi is here."

"Dismiss it," Vicente ordered. "Señorita Harper has changed her mind. She isn't leaving today." He took his wallet from his back pocket and handed some bills to Luisa.

"No!" Alex shouted to Luisa. Her eyes shifted to Vicente. "I can't stay."

"Dismiss the taxi," Vicente repeated in a no-nonsense tone, and the maid left to do as he instructed.

"If I want to go home, I will. My family is expecting me, and in two hours I'll be on a plane back to the United States, with or without your cooperation. Since you've sent my transportation away, then you can take me to the airport yourself."

Vicente, apparently amused by her outburst, grabbed her hand and brought it to his lips. "And if I refuse?"

She yanked her hand away. "Then I'll call another cab."

"Which I'll also dismiss."

"Then I'll walk."

"In the rain? The airport is miles away, and I can see to it that you'll never make your flight in time. Even if you did, it would be futile—I took the liberty of canceling your reservation a few hours ago."

"*You what?*"

He smiled triumphantly. "I canceled your reservation. I told them you had a medical emergency and needed to stay another week."

Alex felt her level of frustration reach the point of eruption. He was back to his old self—controlling, domineering. "So I'll tell them I recovered sooner than expected," she said defiantly. "I may not get away today, but I will tomorrow."

"No, Alex. I'm afraid I can't let you do that."

"Why would you possibly want me to stay? Salinas was a disaster and you've been avoiding—"

"Hardly a disaster," he interrupted. "More of a revelation. You see, as much as you've complicated my life, I find I simply can't allow you to leave."

His words brought a glimmer of hope. "And how do you propose to keep me here?" Her words were soft, questioning.

"As you know, I talked with my father last night. He suggested I use the only weapon at my command—I plan to introduce you to Camila Zavala."

Alex sighed. An introduction to the writer was the last thing she'd expected, and not at all what she wanted from him. Right now she wanted words of love, not some hastily contrived pledge to produce Camila. "Oh, please, not again," she said sharply. "Such an obvious subterfuge, and one you've already attempted."

"I promise you'll meet Camila today at my father's hacienda. We can go there later this morning."

Alex looked at him skeptically. "Why not now? I'm ready."

"You'll have to agree it's rather early to be dropping in."

She checked her watch, then nodded. They couldn't go rousing Juan Carlos from his bed, even if he *was* Vicente's father. Besides, Alex wasn't as ready as she thought she was. First, she needed to call her parents and tell them about the delay. Her parents were early risers. They were probably in the kitchen having coffee about now, unless her father was off on some trip. She hoped Scott was at home. She needed his advice about this new development.

Her father was the one who answered the phone. "Honey, I don't know what to think," he said. "When Juan Carlos suggested her book, I never made any connection with his family. I would have told you if I had. But it sounds like you're finally going to find out everything you want to know." Their phone call then shifted to her activities in Ecuador and the latest antics of her nieces and nephews. It was a full thirty minutes before she hung up.

Alex had assumed that her father had no inkling of Camila's ties to the Serrano family. But she couldn't help wishing he'd been able to enlighten her on what to expect at the hacienda.

During the call, Luisa had laid out a generous breakfast, prepared in spite of Alex's protests. Vicente eagerly filled his plate with hearty portions of eggs, toast, sweet rolls and mixed fruit, then tried to coax her to join him. But she had no appetite. There was no room in her stomach for food with all the nervous tension she was harboring.

The rain clouds had disappeared and the sun was beating down, causing vapor plumes to rise from the wet pavement, when they finally drove away from the estate. Vicente remained quiet as they cleared the Quito traffic and started making their way through the small villages that flanked the southbound highway. He had showered and shaved and changed into fresh clothing, which left him looking less tired and haggard.

Now that she'd had time to think about it, Alex was excited about meeting Camila. But she was also wary. Vicente had seemed anxious for her to go home, so what had caused him to change his mind? Was this latest excursion his idea, or had Juan Carlos insisted that he tell her the truth? She glanced at Vicente. He seemed preoccupied. Now that they were on their way, was he contemplating reneging on his promise? Would this just be another wild-goose chase? But why would he go to such lengths? There was no longer a need for diversion.

They were turning into the hacienda drive when Alex finally got up the nerve to ask the question she'd been ready to pose for the past thirty minutes. "Why is Camila at the hacienda?"

"Wait and see." He glanced her way, his expression serious. "But keep in mind that you could be disappointed. Camila may not live up to your expectations."

"Believe me, I've thought about that a lot recently. I'm looking forward to meeting her, but..."

He stopped the car in front of the house, turning off the engine, then twisting in the seat to face her. "But you're afraid your image of her will be spoiled."

"Something like that. For so long I've felt as though we were kindred souls. I feel it even more now that I've visited Ecuador. I've looked out my window at night, staring at the lights over Quito and wondering where

Camila was, what she was doing, what she was thinking." Alex shook her head ruefully. "Other times—" she stopped. "You probably think I'm a simpleton."

"Right now all I'm thinking is how beautiful you are. How special."

Although he made no attempt to touch her, his words were a caress. But the sensation quickly passed and once again she was anxious. He didn't love her, so why couldn't he have left well enough alone? The sounds of footsteps on the graveled drive rescued her. She didn't have time to react further.

Juan Carlos assisted her from the car, kissing her on the cheek and welcoming her back to his home. "How wonderful to have you return—"

Vicente interrupted the exchange, nodding to his father rather grimly and announcing, "As you suggested, I've brought Alex here to tell her about Camila."

His father also nodded as if unsurprised, and with his hand at Alex's back escorted her inside. No sooner were they over the threshold than Vicente took leave of Juan Carlos, then reached for her elbow and led her to a room off the center hallway. He pulled a key chain from his pocket and unlocked the door, motioning her to enter.

The room, a study, had a feminine look to it, with a set of Queen Anne chairs, a damask love seat and a lingering fragrance of some exotic perfume. In one corner stood an antique secretary, and on an inlaid desk by the window sat an old manual typewriter.

Bookshelves covered two walls, several shelves filled with copies of Camila's books in various languages.

"I don't understand." She looked to him for explanation.

"The Camila you are searching for was my mother Elena," he said bluntly. "This was her office and the materials in here ought to give you many of the answers you've been seeking. She was very fond of you, Alex. Your letters were important to her."

"You knew about the letters?"

"*Sí.* I knew everything." He tenderly raked his knuckles across her chin. "We'll talk of it later. Now, stay here as long as you wish. I'll have some tea brought to you." Vicente disappeared out the door, closing it behind him.

For long moments, Alex stared, transfixed. On the drive down, she'd run through various scenarios in her mind. All of them had to do with meeting someone. She'd been totally unprepared for this.

A tear trickled down her cheek. What did it mean? And why had Vicente decided to tell her? Because he felt guilty? He knew she'd fallen in love with him and was trying to compensate for not returning her love. But she didn't want to think about Vicente any more. As she'd done so often recently, Alex willfully forced her thoughts from him. It helped that the presence of Camila was too overwhelming to ignore.

At first Alex tentatively explored, carefully opening desk drawers to peek inside, poking into the cubicles of the secretary, gazing through the sheer curtains at the view of Cotopaxi. She found family photograph albums and a set of diaries begun when Elena was a young girl, all carefully labeled with a start and finish date. For some reason, the last several years of Elena's life were missing. Another puzzle. Alex chewed on the temple of her glasses. She doubted that Elena would have suddenly stopped. Were there more volumes that Vicente or Juan Carlos had removed before giving her access to the room?

In addition to the diaries, there were notebooks with pages containing outlines of Camila's early novels, the handwriting so endearingly familiar. Loving her own family as she did, Alex could now understand Vicente's deception and even forgive it.

A maid discreetly entered with tea, then disappeared. Alex stopped her exploring and sipped the tea as she began reading, the scholar part of her teeming with excitement. There was much more here than she'd ever need for the *Newsmakers* piece, or even as supplemental information for her dissertation. This material had the makings of a biography. But how much of it would the Serranos allow her to use?

She kept reading, ideas swirling in her brain. Hours passed and the maid delivered lunch, which Alex ignored. She was too engrossed to think about food.

Time for more exploring. The fourth drawer she opened contained a ribbon-bound packet with the letters she'd written. She couldn't stop the tears from welling up again. Camila had kept her letters, an indication that their correspondence was important to her, just as Vicente had said. The ribbon was a lovely old-fashioned touch from the days when letters were saved and treasured.

The light in the room was growing dim when Juan Carlos tapped on the door and entered. He switched on a couple of lamps. "Won't you come have a bite of dinner?"

Alex brushed her hair off her forehead. "I'm sorry. I didn't realize it was so late." She'd completely lost track of time.

"To be sure, there's a great deal here. One can easily get carried away." He picked up a filigreed letter opener and ran his fingers over the ornate design, the faraway expression on his face telling Alex that his thoughts were on his late wife. He shook his head as though clearing away the memories. "I believe our meal is being served."

At one end of a long rectangular dining table that could easily accommodate twelve, two places were set. Juan Carlos held her chair, then sat down across from her.

"Vicente is not going to be with us? Has he returned to Quito?"

"No, *niña*. He sends his apologies, but he's working."

"And he doesn't want to talk about Camila—about his mother."

"On the contrary, we both love talking about her. We may have buried her, but she is still part of our lives. She was a very special woman. Everyone loved Elena."

"Especially you?"

"Especially me. From the first moment I saw her at age fifteen, I was infatuated. We were both guests at a marriage ceremony at La Cienega."

Alex nodded knowingly. "Her second book was about a wedding there. I wish I'd made an effort to go."

"Then Vicente must take you. After you've finished here, of course. It's only a few miles away and . . . but that's another story."

Alex wanted to ask him so many questions. She particularly wanted to know why they hadn't told her about Elena on her first visit but were willing to now. She guessed there was a great deal more to this than she had uncovered so far. But at the moment she didn't want to push her luck. She'd been given access to Camila's office, to Camila's personal papers, and for the time being, it was enough. Later she would seek more answers.

Throughout the meal, without any prodding from Alex, Juan Carlos talked about his wife. Alex knew what Camila—Elena now, she must remember— looked like from the painting in the grand salon, but Juan Carlos was able to bring the image to life. He told her about his wife's sense of humor, her attention to detail, her affinity for people. The Camila Alex had come to know from her books and letters was reinforced with each recollection.

"But why did her writing start changing?" Alex suspected the answer was in the diaries, especially the later ones. Perhaps Juan Carlos would give her a clue.

But he ignored her question, asking, instead, what she thought of the wine. Ever solicitous, yet evasive. Alex realized she'd just have to be patient, and eventually she would learn the whole truth, she was convinced of it. For the moment, she'd undertake her methodical, chronological reading of the memoirs.

Her own particular style of study was to take things slowly, carefully, gradually building on her knowledge. That way, she understood and retained more. However, in this instance, it was difficult not to give in to curiosity and read the last entries first. It was also difficult not to attempt to wheedle more information from her host.

After dinner, Juan Carlos excused himself. "I can see in your eyes that you want to work a while longer. Your belongings have been placed in the same bedroom as before. Please make yourself at home. Take all the time you wish—stay as long as you like." He put his hands on her shoulders and kissed her goodnight. "Elena looked forward to your letters. She cared about you, *niña*." His words echoed those Vicente had spoken earlier that day. Juan Carlos smiled at her and left.

Alex stopped by the bedroom to get a writing tablet from her briefcase, then returned to Elena's study. There was so much here she had difficulty deciding where to start. The diaries... No, the notebooks.

She opened the top notebook. Page one had only eleven words: I have never been poor, yet poverty is all around me. The compelling words were familiar. The opening lines of Camila's first novel. She jotted down the quote. She'd use it in the *Newsmakers* article, probably in her dissertation, too.

Over the next two days time became meaningless. Alex sifted and poured through documents, reading and taking notes, stopping only for meals or brief walks in the courtyard. The longer she worked, however, the more certain she became that something was amiss. She lay back on the love seat in a temporary respite. Suddenly the answer came to her.

"She didn't write *Caribbean Cartel*," Alex announced, sitting upright. Her audience was the old family cat that was now curled beside her on the love seat. Alex suspected it had been a favorite spot for the animal when Elena was alive. "At least not all of it." The cat opened its eyes briefly, decided he'd heard nothing of interest and shut them again. "Don't ignore me," Alex said, stroking the feline. "I can prove it."

She walked over to a bookshelf and pulled out an English version of the novel. Certainly, there were passages that were vintage Camila. But what Alex had seen before as the evolving of a writer, she now realized was something entirely different. All of Camila's works—the notebooks, the diaries, her early books— had a similarity, a gentleness. This novel was harsher, more strident.

As sure as she was standing there, Alex knew that Camila had been only a collaborator on *Caribbean Cartel* and that she'd had little or no part in writing *Death of the Amazon*. No wonder Alex had felt perplexed. She was dealing with two authors, not one. So who was the other? Alex suspected that she knew. And the realization made her furious.

CHAPTER EIGHT

ALEX APPROACHED a gardener who was pruning one of the rosebushes. Trying to keep her agitation from showing in her voice, she asked, "Where's the young Señor Serrano?"

The gardener lifted a gloved hand and gestured. Following the direction he'd indicated, she walked across an old carriage yard and passed through an arbor to a pond.

Vicente was there, crouched beside the water, watching a school of wriggling tadpoles. Upon hearing her footsteps, he stood up. "Getting a breath of fresh air?"

"No, still working," she said. "But I need you to clarify something for me. Several diaries appear to be missing. It's difficult to believe that a meticulous diarist like your mother would simply stop writing, yet the journals end several years before her death. There must be more somewhere else."

"Yes, there *are* more."

"And they explain about her cowriter? Do they explain how you became Camila?"

"So you guessed. Yes, I am now Camila Zavala." A hand went to the back of his neck, rubbing the nape. "I was just waiting for the right time to tell you."

"How long were you going to wait—until I made a total fool of myself? How stupid of me not to see it sooner. I suppose I was too caught up in the discovery of that first book when I should have focused on the later ones. I noticed a difference, but I did a rotten job of figuring out the reason." She raised her hands in frustration. "And you... all this time you allowed me to carry on like an idiot. Well, I hope you've enjoyed your little game."

"Not really. I just thought it was necessary."

"You thought it was necessary," she mimicked. "Well, I think you're... you're a..." Alex was too angry to continue. For someone proficient with words, she was having a difficult time getting her brain and tongue in sync. She turned her back to him and gazed off into the distance, trying to control the urge to cry. It wasn't as though Vicente actually owed her the answer. Still, she felt betrayed.

Eventually she wheeled around to face him. "You must have been quite entertained by my pathetic efforts. My inept questioning of everyone, the assumption that Silvia was Camila. All the time you were laughing at me."

"I never laughed."

"Why not? I find it most humorous," she said bitterly.

Vicente took hold of her arms. "Please listen. I'll admit that your visit came as a surprise to me, and at first my only goal was to thwart your efforts at finding out my secret. To complicate matters, my father was aggressively playing matchmaker. I resented and resisted his efforts to throw us together. I tried to resist you, but I could not." He took a strand of her hair and rubbed it between his fingers gently. "Alex, I brought you here to share Camila with you. So that secrets could be put aside. I also brought you here to ask you to become my wife."

Alex was stunned. And more flustered than ever. Retreat seemed appropriate, at least until she had time to gather her thoughts and figure out how to react. Vicente, however, seemed to read her mind, and he reached out to prevent her escape.

She tried unsuccessfully to pull free, but he held on tight, so she shoved him away, putting all her strength into the push. Vicente let go as he staggered backward, flailing his arms as he toppled into the pond with a big splash. The water was shallow, and he quickly sat up and stared at her in amazement. As he attempted to get to his feet, a frog hopped across his chest, startling him and causing him to lose his balance again.

As Vicente tried to rise again and as his body came into full view, Alex could see his trousers discoloring and his green knit pullover beginning to pucker. His hair, usually perfectly coiffed, hung in his face.

Alex hadn't meant for him to fall. She'd only wanted to get away. Now she watched him warily, expecting to see anger. Instead, his expression continued to be one of astonishment as he first looked at her and then down at himself in disbelief.

She fled toward the house, just reaching the middle of the carriage yard when he caught up with her. His grip was unyielding. "Alex—"

"Don't touch me!" she said.

"I can't help myself."

"In a pig's eye." She turned to face him.

"I can see a few more English lessons are in order for me to master all your quaint expressions. However, it doesn't take much imagination to get the point." Vicente loosened his hold.

"Why was it necessary to play out the whole Camila charade? You could have let me check into a hotel, traipse about on my own, discover nothing and go home. Instead you..." Again words failed her.

He brushed a strand of dripping hair from his face. "Instead, I tried to get to know you."

"You tried to interfere."

"That, too. I was torn. You were one of my mother's favorite people. She'd talked about you for years, so taken with your letters and the tales about your life in Oklahoma. Often she invited us to read your correspondence. It was almost as though you were part of our family. She was planning to invite you for a visit when she became ill."

"You could have written, could have told me she was sick, told me when she...when she..." The tears she'd been fighting now escaped, and Alex wiped a fist across her damp cheeks to stop their flow.

"Could I? And what would I have said? I didn't really know Alexandra Harper. There was a chance you'd go straight to the newspapers with the story. Then how could I have continued writing as Camila Zavala?"

"Perhaps I can understand that part, but it's hard to forgive you for the merry chase you've led me on."

"Has it really been so bad? After all, it gave us time to get to know one another. And I do want you to be my wife, *querida*."

The words sounded sweet to the ear, but they didn't override her skepticism. As much as she wanted him to mean them—as much as she *longed* for him to mean them—Alex felt Vicente had ulterior motives. She couldn't dismiss the suspicion that this marriage proposal was another of his diversionary tactics. The fact that he now had no reason to divert her seemed irrelevant. Alex just wasn't ready to trust Vicente. She started walking again.

The staff at the hacienda was discreet—heads came up as they passed, but then quickly ducked again, everyone carrying on with their labors. Vicente followed close behind her as they entered the house and started up the stairway.

Alex was determined to leave the hacienda as soon as possible. It seemed the only choice. She'd accomplished her mission—she'd found Camila. There was nothing more for her here, however much she wished there could be. She wasn't sure how she'd get away, since they were far from the airport, but she'd figure out something.

Vicente stopped her again as they reached the top of the stairs. "I told you the truth, Alex. I do want you to be my wife. There's much we need to discuss if you'll just calm down and listen to me."

"I've been listening to you ever since I arrived in Ecuador, and you've done nothing but deceive me. Pardon me if I have trouble ignoring what you've done in the past, even though you've just proposed."

The proposal had simply come too soon. Perhaps if he'd given her time to deal with the truth about Camila she'd have been able to react coolly and logically. As much as she'd once tried to deny it, Alex knew she was deeply in love with Vicente Serrano. And she didn't believe his reasons for suggesting marriage included love.

They'd known each other only two weeks, hardly enough time to start considering a permanent relationship. And just days ago at the beach, Vicente had been adamant that a relationship between them wouldn't work. What had made him change his mind?

"As I explained, I did what I had to do. I simply couldn't tell you. Surely you understand that. Think about it."

Alex didn't want to think—she just wanted to be rid of him and the feelings he fostered in her.

Once in her bedroom, she leaned over, hands on knees, taking long, measured breaths. Eventually her careful breathing began to relax her, but she needed to regain total control. Alex rummaged through her briefcase, pulled out a small cassette player and put in a Harry Connick, Jr., tape, a reminder of home. She stripped off her clothes and slipped into a robe, then headed in the direction of the bathroom for a good long soak in the tub.

The music and the soothing heat of the bathwater helped her sort through the maze of confusion. Yes, the man had misled her, but he hadn't demeaned her as a person or as a woman. He hadn't suggested some sordid affair, but marriage, for heaven's sake. Why, though? The question wouldn't go away.

She climbed out of the tub, dried off and spread body lotion over her skin, then took a couple of aspirin. It wasn't possible to hide upstairs forever, so she dressed for a walk, deciding to make another trip to see Larry the llama, and take more photos. Perhaps the pictures could be the basis for a children's story about the animal, a Christmas gift for her many nieces and nephews.

LARRY, as much a ham as ever, stood statue still as she took snapshots. She'd replaced her lens cap and turned back toward the hacienda when she saw Vicente coming toward her. He was once again his immaculate self, the wet clothing replaced by cream-colored pants and a freshly ironed shirt.

He smiled at her. "I hadn't realized I would be getting such a temperamental wife." One hand rested on his hip and there was an assessing look on his face.

"Now that your tirade is over, have you come to your senses and decided to marry me, *bella?*"

She stared at him in wonderment. "I've gotten over being angry, and I'm sorry you fell in the pond. But as far as marriage goes...I quite frankly don't know what to say."

"It's simple—just say yes."

Alex had to shake her head at his presumptuousness. Yet, on reflection, she had to admit it was in keeping with everything else he'd done in the brief time she'd known him.

"Is it that hard to form a response?" he asked.

"First tell me why. That's not so simple, is it?" She returned to the fence penning in the llamas, her back to him. "You certainly weren't considering marriage when we were in Salinas."

"No, I'll admit that marriage wasn't what I was thinking about then. But then I can't seem to get Salinas off my mind, either. Why did I ask you to be my wife? I have no trouble with the why of it." He was now beside her. "I can come up with a half-dozen reasons. One, you have a quiet manner." He grinned before adding, "Most of the time, anyway. Two, you're a working woman, not a socialite. I like that. Plus, you're stimulating to be with. We complement each other, and our priorities are the same."

"That's only five. Besides, you don't know my priorities."

"Yes, I do. Even though our meeting is recent, we've been together a great deal during your stay here.

And don't forget, I've read your letters." He touched her shoulder. "You're the woman I've spent a lifetime waiting for. And here's the sixth and most important reason—I love you."

Vicente sounded sincere, but still she was apprehensive. "Likely the most urgent reason is that it's time you marry." Alex couldn't keep the tremble from her voice.

"That's part of it, I admit."

"Marriage would please your father."

"It would."

"Silvia, though, might be quite upset." Alex clutched a rail of the fence, steadying herself.

"Perhaps. But she'll get over it. Silvia has her own agenda."

"Are you sure I'm not the pawn in some ongoing game between you, Juan Carlos and your lady friend?"

"How did you come up with such an idea?"

Alex turned back to confront him. "Because I overheard your conversation in the garden the night of the party. I regret listening, but I did. I heard her pressuring you for a proposal."

Vicente pursed his lips as he studied her. "That explains a great deal. So you were nearby. Well, no matter. That's behind us now."

"Not really," she said. There were still unanswered questions. "I know you're sympathetic to Silvia, yet you want to be free of her demands."

"That's true, and marriage to you would solve the problem of her wanting to be my wife. It would ward off a few other women, as well. But that hardly seems reason enough, does it?"

"Maybe not in itself, but coupled with your father's blessing, it appears you'd gain a great deal from marriage." Alex started back toward the house, wanting to end this conversation.

"And what about you, Alex? Don't you stand to gain, too?" Not to be deterred, he was right behind her.

"Me?"

"Is it so difficult for you to understand?" He sounded annoyed. "To be crass, I'm a wealthy man. You would share those riches."

She shrugged. "Such luxury doesn't hold much appeal for me." While she could appreciate the opulent surroundings, Alex recalled Silvia's description of her own aimless existence, and she had no desire to experience it itself.

"You would be free to write and study with no worry about having to support yourself in the process."

She sighed. "That, I'll confess, is tempting, but still not sufficient reason for us to embark on a hasty marriage."

He turned her toward him and pulled her into his arms. "It's time to stop weighing our options as if we're buying a house or a car. You know why we should marry." Without another word, his lips were

on hers, hungry and urgent. His kiss caught her unaware. At first she was unresponsive, but as the kiss
continued and his caressing fingers massaged her
back, she couldn't help but react.

She savored the feel of his lips on hers, the rough-
ness of his muscled jaw beneath her hand, all the while
telling herself she could stop the embrace when she
was ready. Brave words, but the longer he held her, the
less in charge she felt. When they finally broke apart,
Alex's pulses were racing. She and Vicente stared into
one another's eyes, as if taking the other's measure.
His arms remained locked around her waist.

"Isn't that sufficient reason?" he finally said.

Alex twisted away, taking a couple of steps backward. As shaken as she was, she still managed to pro-
test. "A marriage between us would never work. I
don't belong here."

"I disagree." Vicente moved closer, taking her face
between his hands. "Admit that you've come to love
my country."

"My enchantment with Ecuador is not a reason for
marriage. Besides…" How could she explain? She was
happy with her life, with her studies. Certainly someday she wanted a home and husband and children. But
when contemplating the notion of marriage, she'd
thought of the distant future and never envisioned
anyone like Vicente Serrano as her husband.

"Stop thinking so hard about it, *querida*. You're
ruffling your forehead." He smiled gently and pulled
her back into his arms. "Marry me."

"I can't." She pushed against his chest. "I'm sorry, but I just can't."

"And I can't accept your refusal, but I won't continue to press my case for now. You need time to consider my proposal. So I promise, no more discussion of marriage today. My father's waiting for us to join him for lunch. Shall we?" He offered her his arm.

Vicente kept his promise as the threesome ate. He and Juan Carlos reminisced about Elena, sharing family anecdotes and helping Alex to feel that she hadn't totally missed out on knowing the woman who'd meant so much to all of them.

Unfortunately Juan Carlos still seemed determined to encourage a romance between Alex and Vicente. "It is nice, is it not, being here together? I think you should extend your stay, Alexandra. There is so much for you to learn about Elena. And my son and I both relish having you with us."

"*Papi,*" Vicente grumbled, the softness in his voice making the word no less an admonishment.

Juan Carlos waved his hand in dismissal. "I'm not going to be hushed like a child. I happen to think Alexandra belongs here. For that matter, your mother felt the same way."

Alex couldn't help but sympathize with Vicente as he sat there trapped between two opposing forces—a father pushing a relationship with a woman who was rejecting that very thing. Obviously Vicente could have silenced his father by telling him that he'd asked Alex to marry him. But he didn't. She admired him for his restraint.

Eventually Vicente was successful in deflecting his father's interest and once again talk centered on Elena. A dessert of creamy mango ice cream had just been served when, at his father's behest, Vicente left to fetch a photograph album filled with his parents' wedding pictures.

Juan Carlos placed his hand over Alex's. "I'm so happy you came back, *niña*. Now if you'll only give Vicente some time to recognize his feelings."

She couldn't let this go on. "Please—you need to understand. It is not Vicente. He asked me to be his wife this morning—"

Before she could say more, Juan Carlos was on his feet, coming around the table to embrace her. "My prayers are answered!" He took the chair beside her. "I have been so worried. Vicente needs someone. He needs you. With you, my son can pursue the labors he enjoys most—his business activities—and still be able to keep his promise to his mother, fulfill her dream."

"Her dream? I don't understand."

"Vicente is hesitant to discuss it. He loved writing with Elena, more because it gave them an opportunity to share something, I think, than his own desire to be a novelist. Elena's career was her own, until, by necessity, he became part of it.

"On her deathbed, he vowed to her that Camila Zavala would live, that the writing would continue. He has kept his word, but it has been a tremendous bur-

den. He works too hard and there has been no one to
ease the load. With your talent, your writing skill, he
can once again be a part of Camila Zavala, but not the
whole.''

Juan Carlos squeezed her hand. "I will be de-
lighted to have you join our family, my dear. She never
told Vicente, but it was Elena's fondest wish that the
two of you would meet and fall in love, and now it's
happened. She never could have imagined you taking
over as Camila Zavala, but I'm sure she would have
approved. And I know Vicente will willingly relin-
quish the role.''

Was that the impetus for Vicente's marriage proposal? That she become Camila? Alex couldn't
fathom such a thing. Surely her prose would never
equal Elena's. Yet she now suspected that the real
reason for the suggested marriage might have finally
been revealed. Just because Vicente had talent, that
didn't mean he wanted to continue writing. Juan Carlos said it was a burden. Did Vicente need a way to
help him keep his deathbed promise? Was finding a
surrogate writer such as her the way?

"I haven't agreed," Alex told Juan Carlos, wanting to end this conversation before Vicente returned.

"But you will." The older man's faith seemed un-
shaken. In this he was much like his son. Once they
decided something, they were determined it would
happen.

He glanced up to see Vicente headed toward them.
"We'll talk no more of it until you're ready." He pat-

ted her hand and rose to take one of the albums from Vicente. The next hour was spent poring over the photographs, then Juan Carlos excused himself for a siesta.

"What were you and my father talking so seriously about?" Vicente asked as soon as his father had left.

"Simply a reporter grilling a subject," Alex's voice was brittle now, "and learning the most interesting things. I didn't realize you were searching for another Camila."

Vicente ran a finger around the rim of his water glass. "My father has been indiscreet."

"Something one would never accuse you of. Why didn't you tell me the truth? Why wrap up your proposal in pretty words when all you were really looking for was someone to ghostwrite the Camila novels?"

"That is not necessarily the situation."

"Why does the word 'necessarily' give me pause?"

"Alex, you don't understand—"

"I understand perfectly. You, Señor Serrano, are the one who doesn't understand. I will not marry you simply to make your life easier. As soon as I can get away, I plan to return home and write my article for *Newsmakers*. It'll be ever so interesting with what I've learned...." Her voice trailed off with the implicit threat.

"I don't believe you," he said. "I know you, Alex. You won't use Camila for personal gain. You won't."

"Oh? Just wait and see."

CHAPTER NINE

ALEX WISHED she'd never heard of Camila Zavala. What had once brought her joy now only brought pain. She'd learned almost everything she wanted to know, and with the knowledge, her life would never again be the same.

Alex was in Elena's study, trying to finish her research. The old manuscripts and diaries couldn't keep her attention anymore. She was too caught up in her own life.

Even after her angry outburst, Vicente had not prevented her from coming here. Of course he hadn't told her where the missing diaries were, either. She'd spent most of the past evening in the study, even skipping dinner, then with a cup of coffee in hand, was back at Elena's desk before sunrise. Sleep had eluded her—for a variety of reasons.

She regretted losing her temper and knew she'd overreacted. It hurt, though, to realize that love hadn't been the reason for Vicente's proposal. She wanted him to mean it when he said he loved her. She wanted to stay in Ecuador, to stay with him. But she couldn't—not without love. So she'd leave as soon as possible. More delay would only increase her misery. That decided, she left the study in search of Vicente.

He was working with one of the laborers, pruning limbs from tomatillo trees.

"I'd like to go back to Quito and arrange my return home."

He climbed down the stepladder. "As you wish." His tone was resigned, as if he'd anticipated her request. She had expected him to argue, maybe even hoped he would. Why else, she mused in bewilderment, did his agreeing to her request cause sadness to grip her heart? This was what was best—wasn't it?

"I'll arrange for someone to pack your luggage. While I change clothes, you can say your farewells to my father." He gestured toward the patio, where Juan Carlos was reading in a lounge chair, an umbrella shading him from the unrelenting afternoon sun.

The older man jumped slightly when she approached.

"I didn't mean to startle you, but—" She stopped abruptly, surprised at the book in his hands. It was *Death of the Amazon.*

"Don't apologize." He motioned her to an adjoining chair. "It wasn't your fault. I was so caught up in the novel I didn't hear you coming. It's the first time I've read it." He quickly interpreted her questioning expression. "It was too painful even to consider—a Camila book with none of Elena." He smiled proudly. "She would have been so pleased with it—with him. The novel is quite magnificent, is it not?"

"Yes, it is. And I'll leave you to it in a moment. But I wanted to say goodbye. I'm going home."

"Surely not goodbye forever?"

She nodded.

Tucking a marker between the pages, he laid the book on the table beside him. "But it is delightful here, don't you agree?"

"I do. And I've loved being here. My only regret is not getting to meet Elena."

Juan Carlos's dark eyes softened, his thoughts clearly drifting to another time. "As I told you, I loved her the moment I saw her. From that day forward there was never another woman in my life. That's how it is with Serrano men, you know."

A maid appeared, placing glasses and a pitcher of lemonade on the table. Juan Carlos smiled as he filled a glass and passed it to Alex.

She accepted reluctantly, wanting to leave, to be free of Vicente and his powerful allure. But she relished Juan Carlos's company and the stories he told. What difference would a few extra minutes make?

"Tell me more about her," she encouraged, recognizing that the older man needed to talk about his wife. No more prompting was necessary, and Juan Carlos spent the next half hour rhapsodizing about his Elena. He was describing their honeymoon in Europe when Vicente joined them.

"Your bags are in the car." He handed Alex her purse.

*So much for wanting to marry me. Now he's be-
having as though he can't wait to get rid of me.*

The next moments were awkward. Saying goodbye
to Juan Carlos and taking her leave of the enchant-
ingly beautiful hacienda were more distressing than
she could have imagined. The cook and maids came
out to wish her well and one of the gardeners also
walked over. *"Vaya con Dios, señorita,"* he said, then
returned to weeding a patch of green lawn. Juan Carlos kissed her cheek and opened the car door. Vicente
was already waiting in the driver's seat.

When they reached the highway, Vicente turned left,
in the opposite direction from Quito.

She sighed. "Where are we going now?"

"A short side trip. My father reminded me that you
haven't been to La Cienega. It's only a few miles from
here."

Once again the controlling male had taken over, but
Alex resigned herself. This was the last time he would
try to control her. Besides, she had wanted to see the
majestic residence that was now used as a hotel and
conference site. In truth, though, it was more than
that. Alex knew going home was the right thing to do,
but she wasn't really ready to leave Vicente. A side trip
would buy her a little time before the final farewell.

"Do you notice the similarity?" he asked as they
pulled through a gate.

Alex nodded. With its whitewashed walls and tree-
lined drive, Vicente's home was a smaller version of
this magnificent mansion. She recognized the trees as

eucalyptus and rolled down the car window to inhale the fragrant scent, but this variety did not have the unique aroma of the more familiar Australian version.

"La Cienega predates our hacienda by at least a hundred years. Family lore says that one of my great-grandmothers first met my great-grandfather in the chapel here. And as you know, that's where my father and mother also met."

He led her into the lobby, stopping for a moment to greet the manager, before leading her through the inner patio to a set of massive carved wooden doors. One door was ajar, and they opened it to enter a family chapel, which was large enough to hold approximately a hundred people. The chapel had stone floors and rows of pews divided by a center aisle. Spaced along newly painted side walls were the stations of the cross. "This has been the site of Serrano weddings for two centuries," Vicente said.

As Alex moved slowly down the aisle, she could imagine herself in a white gown and veil walking toward her groom—walking toward Vicente. For the first time, he was the husband she saw in her mind. Her musings were so intense that she was startled when he took her elbow and led her back outside.

After a brief tour of the grounds, she looked at her watch. "I think it's time to leave."

Vicente shook his head. "Your luggage has been taken upstairs." He paused meaningfully. "I will return for you tomorrow."

If she'd been five instead of twenty-five, Alex would have thrown a full-fledged tantrum. "This is ridiculous! I told you I wanted to go back to Quito." She was totally, irrevocably exasperated with the man. Leaving was consuming all her strength and energy as it was. She doubted she was strong enough to endure another day. "Take me there right now or I promise you I will not be waiting here tomorrow."

Vicente seemed to sense that she was completely serious. "Please, Alex, humor me." His voice was strained with tension. "Don't rush back to the States without taking time to fully consider my offer of marriage. La Cienega will provide a lovely setting for you to do so. Perhaps the magic of the place will work its spell on you. Please, will you stay?"

She wasn't certain whether she was making a wise decision, but all of a sudden Alex knew she couldn't refuse him. Not when his eyes were looking so woeful and his face was showing so much vulnerability. She nodded. "I'll stay."

A glimmer of happiness crossed Vicente's face and he kissed her quickly. "Until tomorrow."

Alex watched his car drive away, then stopped by the front desk to pick up the key to her room. She was exhausted from lack of sleep and her emotional turmoil. Nothing seemed more appealing than the chance to hide somewhere and lock the world out.

Just as Vicente had said, her luggage was waiting inside the door. What he hadn't said was that she'd be staying in the bridal suite, which contained the biggest bed she'd ever seen. It was a canopy bed connected by four massive bedposts and was so tall she needed steps to climb into it. There was a brown cardboard carton lying on the bed. Alex approached dubiously—as if something foul might spring out of the box at any second—and climbed the two steps up to the mattress. Wondering if she was making her own bargain with the Devil, she pulled the carton toward her and opened the lid. Her eyes widened. The missing diaries.

Alex sat on the edge of the bed, one leg folded under her, and skimmed through the pages. There was Elena's entry on the day she discovered she was ill, then the good and bad moments of the malignancy's progression were chronicled. Surprisingly, the memoirs weren't filled with tragic recollections. There was sadness, yes, but mostly there was joy and love—the unyielding support of Juan Carlos, the good-natured disagreements with her son over particular passages in *Caribbean Cartel,* her pride in his literary talent.

In the last year of Elena's life, the entries became fewer and fewer until they finally stopped. Alex rose from the bed and stretched, hands massaging the small of her back. Despite her impulsive threat to Vicente, she knew that little of this material would find its way into her published materials—not her dissertation and most certainly not the *Newsmakers* article. It was too personal, too private.

Venturing downstairs to the bar, she purchased a ginger ale, then returned to her room. She was about to replace the diaries in the box when she noticed a sheaf of papers at the bottom. Setting the diaries aside, she removed the papers, a manuscript, from the box. *Hector's Bride,* by Camila Zavala. The dedication read: "To Hector's inspiration." She carried the manuscript over to an armchair and began to read.

It was almost four in the morning when Alex turned the last page. Tears were streaming from her eyes. *Hector's Bride* was a love story, but more than that, it was a love letter to her from Vicente. The dedication said it all, confirmed by the striking similarities between herself and Consuelo, the heroine.

At that moment her doubts about a life with Vicente vanished. So what if their days together had been so few? True love didn't run according to the clock. And this book convinced Alex that Vicente *did* love her. So what if he anticipated her working with him? She should have considered his asking her to share his brilliant future as a novelist an honor.

Her hand reached for the phone. She wanted to call him. No sooner had she dialed the first digit than reason surfaced. Everyone would be asleep. A ringing telephone would awaken Juan Carlos and disrupt the entire household.

But how she longed to talk with Vicente, to hear his voice. She dabbed at her eyes and stood up again, twisting to and fro, trying to relieve muscles cramped from sitting too long. Frustrated by the prospect of her impending wait, she picked up her overnight bag and removed a pair of pajamas and her makeup kit, then went to the bathroom. Maybe sleep would make the time pass more quickly.

But once she climbed into that enormous bed all she could focus on was Vicente. She desperately wanted him to be there, holding her in his arms, making love to her. Yet such fixations made Alex's fears resurface. *Hector's Bride* was a glorious tale, but had a wonderfully crafted piece of fiction read in a romantic setting clouded her judgment?

Why did love have to be full of complications? She couldn't help thinking of her family. Her parents and sisters had always been close, and when life took an important turn they were on hand. If she married Vicente, that closeness would no longer be possible. Quito was depressingly far from home. How could she ever hope to keep up with all the separate households from such a distance? She'd miss out on such day-to-day activities as family dinners and gossip with her sisters. She'd miss the special occasions—birthday parties and baby showers. Alex knew her life would be forever changed. She felt a stab of melancholy as she saw the door closing on her past.

Yet what really mattered was that Alex loved Vicente Serrano. Her feelings were not just based on attraction or desire, but something more. How it happened, or when, she didn't know exactly. But it had. She would love him for the rest of her life. And at last she was able to accept it. If he asked her to marry him again, she would say yes. He'd spoken about the magic of La Cienega. She decided that something magical had happened to her.

Eventually she drifted off to sleep, and when she awoke it was with surprise to discover that she'd slept most of the morning away. Knowing that Vicente would likely be here before long, she quickly dressed and went downstairs to the dining room. She was famished, having been so absorbed with the novel the night before that she'd skipped dinner for the second time in a row. She ordered a basket of warm breads and a compote of fresh fruits, along with a cup of tea. Each time she heard a footfall, she looked up to see if Vicente had arrived, and each time she was disappointed.

Breakfast over, she decided to stop waiting around like a helpless female and call him. The maid informed her that he'd gone out. Alex decided he must be on his way, and so she freshened her makeup. Then she sat in a chair by the open window overlooking the front courtyard where she could see him arrive.

It was a Hollywood-perfect day—a cloudless technicolor blue sky, birds chirping contentedly from overhanging tree limbs and a pleasing fragrance drifting up from the flowering bushes below. The only thing not right with the world was Alex. Her insecurities about Vicente were threatening to resurface, and her nerves knotted more tightly with every passing second. Where was he? She glanced at her watch—only ten minutes had passed since her telephone call and the drive would take Vicente at least thirty. She tried to will herself to relax.

Moments later she let out a breath of relief. Vicente's car was coming up the drive. After checking her appearance again, Alex hurried to meet him. But at the top of the staircase, she paused, trying to see if he had the same feelings. No second glance was necessary.

She ran down the steps, and they stared at one another for a few moments. Then she smiled at him, a smile that said "I love you."

"*Mi amor.*" Vicente pulled her to him, kissing her briefly then squeezing her breathless in a long hug of happiness. He looped an arm around her shoulder. "Why don't we stroll outside where it's more private?" As soon as they were out of hearing of the hotel staff, he spoke again. "Marry me here at La Cienega, Alex. A big wedding—we'll have all your family come down."

"Are you sure you're ready for so many Harpers?"

"I've met two already—Scott, whom I'm very fond of, and you...." He nuzzled her behind the ear. "I may fall in love with the whole family." He folded her arm in his and led her to a secluded bench where he could give her the sort of kiss more appropriate for an engagement.

As the kiss ended, she pulled back, a slight frown on her face. "*Hector's Bride* is beautiful. I couldn't put it down. But what about Camila? That's the one matter we haven't fully resolved.''

"Alex, before you arrived, I was dismayed that you were about to intrude in my life, a life that already had too many demands on it. Admittedly I was curious to meet you, but the timing was all wrong. I had a deadline from the publisher, and business demands were unceasing. To make matters worse, my father insisted that you stay at Casa Serrano as a gesture of hospitality because you were Scott Harper's daughter—at least that's what he kept saying. I suspected it was really because of the letters, but I reluctantly agreed to meet you.

"Then you walked out of the airport terminal and my negative thoughts were all but forgotten. Like my father and grandfathers before me, I think I fell in love at that very moment—which irritated me all the more. If I didn't have time for guests, I certainly didn't have time for love. So while the passionate side of me wanted you close by, the rational side demanded I deny my feelings.

"All my life I've heard how Serrano men knew their women from the instant their eyes first met. Frankly I'd been disbelieving and I decided to attribute my feelings for you to the power of suggestion. I kept telling myself that all you wanted was to get to Camila, to use her and expose her. Perhaps I was behaving like a rebellious adolescent. My father was pressuring me and my mother had been proclaiming your virtues for years. I think she'd always hoped we'd meet and fall in love.''

''Your father told me the same thing,'' Alex murmured. ''I wish I'd known her. I wish she were here now.''

''She is. I feel her presence. She's happy with the woman I've chosen.'' His arm drew her closer and he kissed her again. A carpenter, repairing a broken window, dropped a tool, making them aware they were not alone in the courtyard. Vicente pulled her to her feet and led her to the chapel, shutting the huge door behind them.

He reached into his pocket. ''I brought this up from the hacienda. It's been in a safe there.'' He opened a small black velvet box and took out a ring, a heart-shaped diamond surrounded by emeralds.

Vicente lifted her left hand and slipped the ring on to her finger. The fit was perfect. ''Do you like it, *querida?*''

''It's magnificent.'' She held up her hand and wriggled her fingers to catch a sunbeam from the window.

Vicente's face eased into a sad smile. ''My father gave it to my mother for their twenty-fifth wedding anniversary. During her final days, she passed it on to me—as an engagement ring for my future wife. So will there be a wedding, Alex?'' They walked a few steps toward the altar.

His voice was calm, firm, yet it couldn't hide his vulnerability. There was no doubt about his love now.

Alex turned. "I love you, Vicente Serrano. I would be honored to be your wife."

"And not just because of Camila?"

"How can you say—?"

"Shh," he said gently. "I didn't mean to offend you, but I had to clear all doubts from my mind."

"I love you. There is no other reason."

"I know you have obligations and I defer to them. You must first complete the *Newsmakers* feature before we start planning our wedding. After we're married you can finish your dissertation, then we'll undertake a new Camila novel. Just promise me you'll stay in Ecuador. And that you'll help me keep Camila the enigma she is."

"I promise."

"I never intended to tell you, you know." He spoke gently, his newfound candor refreshing to Alex. "I was trying to work on *Hector's Bride*—the idea was there, but it hadn't gone well from the start. Then you arrived and distracted me even more than I already was. I thought I could put you off. Instead, you changed my life. Everything that had been missing from the novel was suddenly in focus. I was unable to write about love before, because I had not yet discovered it for myself."

They were now at the end of the aisle, the aisle Alex knew she would be walking down as Vicente's bride.

He took her hand and brought it to his lips. *"Te amo, mi esposa, mi vida."* I love you, my wife, my life. Alex knew his words were a vow. In searching for Camila, she had found her future.

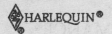 HARLEQUIN®  Silhouette®

The movie event of the season can be the reading event of the year!

Lights... The lights go on in October when CBS presents Harlequin/Silhouette Sunday Matinee Movies. These four movies are based on bestselling Harlequin and Silhouette novels.

Camera... As the cameras roll, be the first to read the original novels the movies are based on!

Action... Through this offer, you can have these books sent directly to you! Just fill in the order form below and you could be reading the books...before the movie!

48288-4	Treacherous Beauties by Cheryl Emerson	$3.99 U.S./$4.50 CAN.	☐
83305-9	Fantasy Man by Sharon Green	$3.99 U.S./$4.50 CAN.	☐
48289-2	A Change of Place by Tracy Sinclair	$3.99 U.S./$4.50CAN.	☐
83306-7	Another Woman by Margot Dalton	$3.99 U.S./$4.50 CAN.	☐

TOTAL AMOUNT	$
POSTAGE & HANDLING	$
($1.00 for one book, 50¢ for each additional)	
APPLICABLE TAXES*	$ _____
<u>**TOTAL PAYABLE**</u>	$ _____
(check or money order—please do not send cash)	

To order, complete this form and send it, along with a check or money order for the total above, payable to Harlequin Books, to: **In the U.S.:** 3010 Walden Avenue, P.O. Box 9047, Buffalo, NY 14269-9047; **In Canada:** P.O. Box 613, Fort Erie, Ontario, L2A 5X3.

Name: _____

Address: _____ City: _____

State/Prov.: _____ Zip/Postal Code: _____

*New York residents remit applicable sales taxes.
  Canadian residents remit applicable GST and provincial taxes.

CBSPR

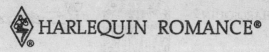

HARLEQUIN ROMANCE®

brings you

Stories that celebrate love, families and children!

Watch for our next Kids & Kisses title in November!

Who's Holding the Baby?
by Day Leclaire
Harlequin Romance #3338

Everybody loves this baby—but who's supposed to be looking after her? A delightful and very funny romance from the author of To Catch a Ghost *and* Once A Cowboy....

Toni's only three months old, and already she needs a scorecard to keep track of the people in her life! She's been temporarily left with her uncle Luc, who's recruited his secretary Grace, who's pretending to be his fiancée, hoping to mollify the police, who've called the child-welfare people, who believe that Grace and Luc are married! And then life starts to get *really* complicated....

Available wherever Harlequin books are sold.

EDGE OF ETERNITY
Jasmine Cresswell

Two years after their divorce, David Powell
and Eve Graham met again in Eternity,
Massachusetts—and this time there was magic
between them. But David was tied up in a
murder that no amount of small-town gossip
could free him from. When Eve was pulled into
the frenzy, he knew he had to come up with
some answers—including how to convince her
they should marry again...this time for keeps.

EDGE OF ETERNITY, available in
November from Intrigue, is the sixth book in
Harlequin's exciting new cross-line series,
WEDDINGS, INC.

Be sure to look for the final book, **VOWS,** by
Margaret Moore (Harlequin Historical #248),
coming in December.

"HOORAY FOR HOLLYWOOD" SWEEPSTAKES

HERE'S HOW THE SWEEPSTAKES WORKS

OFFICIAL RULES — NO PURCHASE NECESSARY

To enter, complete an Official Entry Form or hand print on a 3" x 5" card the words "HOORAY FOR HOLLYWOOD", your name and address and mail your entry in the pre-addressed envelope (if provided) or to: "Hooray for Hollywood" Sweepstakes, P.O. Box 9076, Buffalo, NY 14269-9076 or "Hooray for Hollywood" Sweepstakes, P.O. Box 637, Fort Erie, Ontario L2A 5X3. Entries must be sent via First Class Mail and be received no later than 12/31/94. No liability is assumed for lost, late or misdirected mail.

Winners will be selected in random drawings to be conducted no later than January 31, 1995 from all eligible entries received.

Grand Prize: A 7-day/6-night trip for 2 to Los Angeles, CA including round trip air transportation from commercial airport nearest winner's residence, accommodations at the Regent Beverly Wilshire Hotel, free rental car, and $1,000 spending money. (Approximate prize value which will vary dependent upon winner's residence: $5,400.00 U.S.); 500 Second Prizes: A pair of "Hollywood Star" sunglasses (prize value: $9.95 U.S. each). Winner selection is under the supervision of D.L. Blair, Inc., an independent judging organization, whose decisions are final. Grand Prize travelers must sign and return a release of liability prior to traveling. Trip must be taken by 2/1/96 and is subject to airline schedules and accommodations availability.

Sweepstakes offer is open to residents of the U.S. (except Puerto Rico) and Canada who are 18 years of age or older, except employees and immediate family members of Harlequin Enterprises, Ltd., its affiliates, subsidiaries, and all agencies, entities or persons connected with the use, marketing or conduct of this sweepstakes. All federal, state, provincial, municipal and local laws apply. Offer void wherever prohibited by law. Taxes and/or duties are the sole responsibility of the winners. Any litigation within the province of Quebec respecting the conduct and awarding of prizes may be submitted to the Regie des loteries et courses du Quebec. All prizes will be awarded; winners will be notified by mail. No substitution of prizes are permitted. Odds of winning are dependent upon the number of eligible entries received.

Potential grand prize winner must sign and return an Affidavit of Eligibility within 30 days of notification. In the event of non-compliance within this time period, prize may be awarded to an alternate winner. Prize notification returned as undeliverable may result in the awarding of prize to an alternate winner. By acceptance of their prize, winners consent to use of their names, photographs, or likenesses for purpose of advertising, trade and promotion on behalf of Harlequin Enterprises, Ltd., without further compensation unless prohibited by law. A Canadian winner must correctly answer an arithmetical skill-testing question in order to be awarded the prize.

For a list of winners (available after 2/28/95), send a separate stamped, self-addressed envelope to: Hooray for Hollywood Sweepstakes 3252 Winners, P.O. Box 4200, Blair, NE 68009.

CBSRLS

OFFICIAL ENTRY COUPON

"Hooray for Hollywood"
SWEEPSTAKES!

Yes, I'd love to win the Grand Prize — a vacation in Hollywood — or one of 500 pairs of "sunglasses of the stars"! Please enter me in the sweepstakes!

This entry must be received by December 31, 1994.
Winners will be notified by January 31, 1995.

Name _____

Address _____ Apt. _____

City _____

State/Prov. _____ Zip/Postal Code _____

Daytime phone number _____
(area code)

Mail all entries to: Hooray for Hollywood Sweepstakes,
P.O. Box 9076, Buffalo, NY 14269-9076.
In Canada, mail to: Hooray for Hollywood Sweepstakes,
P.O. Box 637, Fort Erie, ON L2A 5X3.

KCH

IT'S FREE! IT'S FUN! ENTER THE

☆ "Hooray for ☆
☆ Hollywood"☆

SWEEPSTAKES!

We're giving away prizes to celebrate the screening of four new romance movies on CBS TV this fall! Look for the movies on four Sunday afternoons in October. And be sure to return your Official Entry Coupons to try for a fabulous **vacation in Hollywood!**

 If you're the Grand Prize winner we'll fly you and your companion to Los Angeles for a 7-day/6-night vacation you'll never forget!

 You'll stay at the luxurious Regent Beverly Wilshire Hotel,* a prime location for celebrity spotting!

 You'll have time to visit Universal Studios,* stroll the Hollywood Walk of Fame, check out celebrities' footprints at Mann's Chinese Theater, ride a trolley to see the homes of the stars, and more!

 The prize includes a rental car for 7 days and $1,000.00 pocket money!

Someone's going to win this fabulous prize, and it might just be you! Remember, the more times you enter, the better your chances of winning!

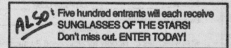

ALSO Five hundred entrants will each receive SUNGLASSES OF THE STARS! Don't miss out. ENTER TODAY!

The proprietors of the trademark are not associated with this promotion.

CBSIBC